P9-APC-714

# Chapter 1

This is a novel written about dolls in a dolls' house. The chief person in it is Tottie Plantaganet, a small Dutch doll.

Dutch dolls are scarce now, but Tottie was made a long time ago when they were plentiful and sold in every shop that had toys for sale; and large ones cost a penny, the middle size a halfpenny, and very small ones, like Tottie, were sold for a farthing each.

At present she lived in the nursery of two little girls called Emily and Charlotte Dane. I say 'at

1

present' because Tottie had lived a long while; once she had lived with two other little girls who were Emily and Charlotte's great-grandmother and their Great-Great-Aunt Laura.

How strange that a little farthing doll should last so long. Tottie was made of wood and it was good wood. She liked to think sometimes of the tree of whose wood she was made, of its strength and of the sap that ran through it and made it bud and put out leaves every spring and summer, that kept it standing through the winter storms and wind. 'A little, a very little of that tree is in me,' said Tottie. 'I am a little of that tree.' She liked to think of it.

She was made of that wood, neatly jointed at the hips and shoulders and sockets (she had sockets for elbows and knees), with a sturdy inch-wide yoke for shoulders and a round little head with glossy painted hair. She had glossy pink cheeks and her eyes were painted with bright firm paint, blue and very determined.

Emily and Charlotte had chosen two other dolls to be Tottie's father and mother; their names were Mr Plantaganet and Mrs Plantaganet, but Mrs Plantaganet had another name and that was Birdie. Of course Tottie knew, just as you and I know, that Mr and Mrs Plantaganet were not her real father and mother, that she had no real father and mother, unless it were that felled tree of whose wood she was made. She knew that, just as she knew that her little brother Apple, the doll they had given her for a little brother, was made from plush (which is a kind of velvet), and Darner, the dolls' house dog, had a backbone made from a darning needle; if you have ever played at Fathers and Mothers, and of course you have played at Fathers and Mothers, you will remember what a very good feeling it is; that was exactly the feeling between Tottie and Mr and Mrs Plantaganet – Birdie – and little brother Apple and Darner the dog.

It is an anxious, sometimes a dangerous thing to be a doll. Dolls cannot choose; they can only be chosen; they cannot 'do'; they can only be done by; children who do not understand this often do wrong things, and then the dolls are hurt and abused and lost; and when this happens dolls cannot speak, nor do anything except be hurt and abused and lost. If you have any dolls, you should remember that.

Listen to the story of Mr Plantaganet (before he was Mr Plantaganet); for a long while he was hurt and abused and lost. He was a delicate little doll, rather larger than Tottie, with a china face and brown glass eyes and real brown hair. He was a boy doll and he always said he remembered once being dressed in a kilt as a Highlander, with toy bagpipes stuck to his hand with hard painful glue, painful when you tried to get it off. He was bought for some children – not, I am glad to say, Emily and Charlotte, quite other children – who took no care of him at all. It was they who dragged the bagpipes off and took some of the painted skin off the palm of his hand as well, and tore his clothes off too, and let their puppy bite his foot until it looked half nibbled. One of the boys drew a moustache on his little top lip with indelible pencil ('indelible' means it can never come off); then they threw him into the cold dark toy cupboard, where he lay for weeks and months and might have lain for years if they had not been ordered to tidy the toy cupboard because children were coming to tea. As it was, they left him lying on the floor under the table and Emily, who was one of the visitors, nearly trod on him.

'Oh! I am sorry,' cried Emily, but nobody seemed to think it mattered. 'What a dear little doll,' said Emily, picking him up. 'Who is he? Whom does he belong to?' He did not seem to belong to anyone.

She noticed that his eyes were filled with dust. The children said Emily could have him, and she wrapped him up in her handkerchief and took him home.

She and Charlotte saw at once that he was made to be a little man doll. They sponged the dust and glue off him with hot water and dried him carefully, and, though the moustache would not come off, they knitted him a sock for his spoilt foot and put plaster on the palm of his hurt hand; and their mother made him a check flannel suit and a blue shirt and a tie of red silk ribbon. Emily cut him tiny newspapers out of the real ones to read.

'I like him with a moustache,' said Emily.

'It makes him look more like Mr Plantaganet,' said Charlotte.

He could still not quite believe he was Mr Plantaganet. He was still easily made afraid, afraid of being hurt or abused again. Really you might have thought that Tottie was the father and he was the child; but there are real fathers like that.

Mrs Plantaganet was not quite right in the head. There was something in her head that rattled; Charlotte thought it might be beads, and it was true that the something made a gay sound

5

like bright beads touching together. She was altogether gay and light, being made of cheap celluloid, but, all the same, nicely moulded and joined and painted.

She came to Charlotte on a cracker at a party. Yes, Mrs Plantaganet started life as part of a cracker, to which she was fastened by silver tinsel. She had been dressed in blue and green feathers. At first they had not thought she was anything more than part of the cracker. First Charlotte kept her on the cracker; then off the cracker; then one day she decided to dress her and pulled the feathers off.

The feathers were glued on Mrs Plantaganet and here was her difference from Mr Plantaganet: the glue coming off did not hurt her at all; it came off easily with hot water, leaving not a trace, and her body only gave out a warm celluloid smell and turned even more pink.

'There is something brave about this little doll,' said Emily. 'I don't usually like celluloid dolls.'

'Nor do I,' said Charlotte. 'But I like her.'

Emily made Mrs Plantaganet a red skirt with blue rickrack braid on the hem, a blue blouse with red spots; the spots were pin spots, but they looked large as buttons to Mrs Plantaganet. 'I think she likes them large and bright,' said Emily. They sewed her hair, which was fluffy yellow cotton, into a bun; but Emily thought again and let the hair out of the bun, loosed and flyaway. 'I think she was wishing we could let it fly away like that,' said Charlotte. 'I think she likes her hair.'

They put her next to Mr Plantaganet and they seemed to suit one another at once. They seemed to suit Tottie too. Tottie had on a little apron that was embroidered with red daisies; both Mr and Mrs Plantaganet thought she looked the very pattern of a nice small wooden girl; they were to think even more of her later.

'We must get Mr Plantaganet a walking stick,' said Emily. 'And Mrs Plantaganet must have a hat with a tiny feather.'

There were still something of the cracker and feather look about Mrs Plantaganet as there was still something of the dark toy cupboard about Mr Plantaganet.

'But Tottie has been ours always,' said Emily.

'Even before always,' said Charlotte.

As for Apple, there were no fears for him. Come fog, come fine, no one could be unkind to Apple. He was as big as Emily's thumb, plump and made of warm plush, coloured pink-brown. He felt nice and he was nice, with chunky little arms and legs and sewn-in dimples and a wig of brown darning-wool hair. Perhaps it was the darning wool that made Darner so fond of him. Apple wore a buster suit, scarlet felt trousers and a white cambric blouse, white socks, and red felt shoes that were fastened with the smallest of small pearl buttons you can imagine. No one ever saw Apple without exclaiming, 'What a little love of a doll!' Tottie and Mr Plantaganet felt that too, through they knew how naughty he was; Birdie, Mrs Plantaganet, felt it, but she did not know that he was ever naughty; she only loved him.

You had to be very careful how you touched Darner because he had a prick at his head end; it was his darning-needle backbone and it made him difficult to handle. The rest of him was clipped wool, gone a little grey with London grime, over pipe-cleaner legs. Emily and Charlotte used to take him, in his turn, as they took the rest of the family, to the Park, where he liked to be stood in the shelter of a fallen leaf (if it were autumn and there were fallen leaves),

so that he could bristle at other and real-size dogs.
He also liked staying at home.

That was the trouble. There was no home.

# Chapter 2

The shortage of dolls' houses was acute.

There were a few in the toyshops but they were very expensive and made of cheap papier-mâché or plywood. 'Not worth the money,' said the children's father. 'They wouldn't last any time.'

'I want one to last,' said Mr Plantaganet with a catch in his breath. 'I want one to last for always.' More than anything in the world Mr Plantaganet wanted a home. 'One that will shut. One that will last. Do you think they will ever buy a house for us?'

he asked. Being a doll, he could not say, 'Do you think we shall ever buy a house?' He had to wait until Emily or Charlotte, or Emily and Charlotte's father, had the idea of buying one for him. Even if they had the idea, these days it was too expensive and he knew that the money Emily and Charlotte put into his pockets was only gold and silver paper. 'I don't think we shall ever have a house,' said Mr Plantaganet.

'One will come. One will come,' sang Birdie.

'How do you know?' asked Mr Plantaganet.

Birdie could not say how she knew. The thought of it rattled in her head with the thought of that tiny raffia hat that Emily had now found for her; it was no bigger than a half-crown and Emily had fixed in it a feather from her aunt's canary. Remembering that, Birdie suddenly remembered what she had thought about the house. 'Emily fixed the hat,' she said. 'Someone will fix the house.'

Of course there were dolls' houses advertised in the newspaper, even sometimes in the part of the newspaper Emily cut up for Mr Plantaganet. *Dolls' houses for sale. Four rooms, fully furnished, electric light, loggia. Garage with miniature cars. £25.*

'That's an enormous heap of money,' said Charlotte.

'But I don't want electric light,' said Mr Plantaganet. 'A little pretending candlestick would do for me, and I wouldn't know how to drive any kind of car.'

But even the plain dolls' houses, *Four rooms . . . Two rooms . . . Some furniture . . .* were seven or eight or three even four guineas each, and neither Emily and Charlotte nor their father had that much money to spare. 'We shall never get one,' said Mr Plantaganet.

At the moment the Plantaganets were as uncomfortable as anyone in London; they had to live crowded together in two shoe-boxes that were cramped and cold and that could not shut; when they hung their washing out to dry, even the smallest pattern duster, it made the cardboard sodden and damp. 'You can't play with them properly,' wailed Charlotte.

'It doesn't feel like home,' said Mr Plantaganet. 'Though of course it is ever so much nicer than the toy cupboard,' he added hastily. 'But I am too heavy for it, and so is Apple. It doesn't feel safe.'

'I don't mind it,' said Birdie, but then Birdie, aggravating creature, never minded anything. She was happy anywhere.

'It slips about. Everybody knocks it over. It doesn't feel safe,' said Mr Plantaganet.

'Long long ago,' began Tottie in her comforting voice (and it is the best wood that gives out the most comforting voice – ask the men who make pianos and violins and flutes), 'long long ago, I knew a dolls' house. I lived in it. It belonged to Laura. She was Emily and Charlotte's great-great-aunt. That was a hundred years ago,' said Tottie.

Tottie had stayed the same all that time, for all that hundred years. Does that surprise you? It is easier for dolls than children. From the moment they are made, finished, they never have to alter, they never have to grow. 'I wouldn't be a child for anything.' Tottie often said. 'First you have to be a baby, then a little child, then a bigger child, then a schoolboy or girl, then a big boy or girl, then grown up.' Of course Tottie knew she could not, even if she would; there is no power of growing in dolls, and she knew that was why, for instance, any live little girl, however stupid, had power over her. 'I am as I am,' said wise little Tottie. 'I couldn't be all those things. In all these years, these hundred years, I can still only be me.' It is very important for dolls that children guess their right ages; some thoughtless children make their dolls vary between six and six months. Mr Plantaganet for instance was born twenty-eight years old. Tottie was about seven. Apple would always be three. Darner was so cross that it was easy to guess he was old. Birdie was more difficult, it was her flightiness, but even Birdie was easily seen to be between twenty and thirty.

'I was telling you about the dolls' house,' said Tottie. 'It was not too big. It could stand comfortably on the table and outside it was a glossy cream colour painted with ivy. It looked as good as real ivy,' said Tottie.

'It would be better than real ivy,' said Mr Plantaganet. 'Real ivy chokes things and can even pull down a house. Painted ivy is safer. I like painted ivy. Go on.'

'Go on. Go on,' cried Apple. Emily had put him on a chair, but he had deliberately fallen off upside down because he wanted to practise standing on his head.

'Don't do that, Apple dear,' said Tottie. 'The dolls' house? Oh, yes. In the front there was a front door with steps leading up to it.'

'How many steps?'

'Six,' said Tottie, 'and the door was painted green with a knocker; it didn't really open but that didn't matter, because the whole of the front swung open, leaving the inside ready to be played with.'

'Leaving the steps?' asked Mr Plantaganet anxiously.

'Leaving the steps,' nodded Tottie, and she added, remembering, 'On the steps was fixed a little tiny scraper.'

'Would my foot go on it?' asked Apple, 'my foot, in its red shoe?'

'Perfectly,' said Tottie. 'And yours,' she said to Mr Plantaganet before he need ask. 'There was a kennel,' she said, 'just outside.'

'For Darner?' asked Apple.

'But would he go in it?' asked Mr Plantaganet doubtfully.

'In this kennel I think he would,' said Tottie.

Darner did not growl as he would have if he had thought the kennel was dangerous. He always growled 'Prrick' at danger.

'There was a hall with a staircase and a polished wooden floor. I remember the floor particularly,' said Tottie, 'because it looked like a draughtboard. Draughts is a game you play on a board checked in squares of light and dark wood,' she explained to Apple. 'The walls of the hall were red. Red paper,' she said, 'that looked like satin.'

'Are you sure it did?' asked Mr Plantaganet doubtfully. 'I haven't seen any paper like that.'

'You would have once,' said Tottie. 'I am quite certain. I remember it looked cosy and rich. There was a hall window with lace curtains; the white looked pretty on the red; there were Christmas scraps for pictures and a clock glued on the wall, and two dolls' house dark wood chairs and a tiny rug.'

'Everything!' said Mr Plantaganet.

'Everything. And in the hall,' said Tottie, 'was the figure of a butler.'

No one asked her why she said 'the figure of a butler' instead of 'a butler'. They knew that whoever had made, or tried to make, that butler had not been successful. There are some dolls like that. There was no need to pity him because he never had been a butler.

'We could put him outside,' said Mr Plantaganet. 'Go on.'

'To the left was the kitchen,' Tottie went on. 'You know which the left is, Apple, your left hand, the one you don't shake hands with. On the left, then, was the kitchen.'

'What was it like?'

'What was it like?'

'What was it like?'

'There was a blue tin stove with sauce-pans and a kettle. There was a heavy iron on a stand, no bigger than Emily's fingernail. There was a rolling pin and a wooden pudding basin smaller than a thimble. There was a dresser with flowered china cups and plates on it, a table and another rug and kitchen chairs and a mangle and a pot of pre-tending geraniums on the window sill.'

'Oh, dear!' said Mr Plantaganet longingly.

Up to now the thought of the house and the thought of her hat had been knocking together in Birdie's head; now she asked, 'Was there a little feather broom?'

'I think there was,' said Tottie.

'Dear!' said Birdie, and the feather broom and the feather in her hat seemed to float before her eyes.

'Could you make buns for tea in that kitchen?' asked Apple. 'What is a bun?'

'To the right of the hall,' said Tottie, 'you know

your right hand, Apple dear, the one you do shake hands with, to the right was a sitting room. It had a green carpet,' said Tottie, 'the colour of holly leaves, and it had real wallpaper, like the hall, only this one was white with cream stripes. On the wallpaper were two little pictures; their frames were made of glued-on shells that Laura had picked up at the seaside. There was another window—'

'Did it open?'

'No, it didn't open, but it had lace curtains too, and there was a fireplace and a fire of shining red gelatine paper. There was a sofa covered in red velvet and two chairs to match, and a table and a piano; its notes were paper notes glued on. On the table,' said Tottie slowly, 'was a lamp with a white china shade; it would really light if you used a birthday cake candle.'

'We should have to be careful of Apple with that candle,' said Birdie suddenly, and they all stared at her because that was such an unusually clear thing for Birdie to say.

'You are right to be afraid of fire,' said Tottie. 'You are celluloid, Birdie, and that would flare up in an instant if you went anywhere near fire.'

'You would, you know,' said Mr Plantaganet. 'Better not go near the candle, Birdie.'

'I?' asked Birdie, surprised. 'I was thinking of Apple.'

'Also on the table,' said Tottie, 'there was a vase of wax roses; they were modelled in wax and they were no bigger than a thimble.'

'Like the pudding basin,' murmured Mr Plantaganet.

'Yes,' said Tottie, 'and in the sitting room there was a golden cage and inside the cage was a bird.'

'A bird?' asked Birdie. 'A-ah! Did it sing?'

'No, it couldn't sing,' said Tottie, 'but it was there.'

'It could sing,' said Birdie, and her eyes seemed to shine. 'I know how it sang.' Scraps and pieces of all the songs she had ever heard knocked together gently in her head with bird songs, chiefly sparrow because she had heard little else, being a London doll; she could not sing any one of them but they all ran together and seemed to make a chain of song in her head such as might be sung by a bright toy bird. 'A-ah! sighed Birdie. Music, delicate clock-work musical-box music, was what Birdie liked to hear.

'Upstairs,' said Tottie, 'there were two bed-rooms. One had a pink flannel carpet and one had a blue. There were beds with nicked-round blankets, and there was a white tin bath with taps, and there was a cot with bars.'

'Would it do for me?' asked Apple.

'It would be a good fit,' said Tottie gravely. 'There was a jug and basin and a pail to match them, for carrying the water downstairs.'

'Very thoughtful,' said Mr Plantaganet. 'Did the taps on the bath really run?'

'Yes, if you put the water in the tank behind the bath,' said Tottie.

Mr Plantaganet nodded. Apple was thinking about the cot. Birdie was thinking about the bird in the birdcage.

'Occupied, of course?' said Mr Plantaganet suddenly.

'Occupied?' asked Tottie.

'I mean there are other dolls living in it, of course?'

'It was a long time ago,' said Tottie. 'Maybe it has gone, been sold or broken up. I don't know where it is now,' said Tottie sadly. 'That Laura, Great-Great-Aunt Laura, had a little girl, but the little girl is a great-aunt herself now. Why, she is Emily and Charlotte's great-aunt. Maybe she has given it away or given it up. I don't know.'

'But dolls lived in it then,' said Mr Plantaganet. 'You lived in it once. Did other dolls live there with you? Don't you remember them?'

'I remember one,' said Tottie slowly. 'Yes, I remember her,' said Tottie, very, very slowly.

'Why do you say it like that? What was her name?'

'Her name was Marchpane.'

'What a funny name. What does it mean?'

'Marchpane is a heavy, sweet, sticky stuff like almond icing, very old-fashioned,' said Tottie. 'You very quickly have enough of it. It was a good name for her,' said Tottie slowly.

'But what was she like?' asked Mr Plantaganet.

'What was she like?' asked Birdie.

'What was she like?' asked Apple.

'She was valuable,' said Tottie. 'She was little and heavy.'

'What was she made of? I am made of celluloid,' said Birdie, and 'celluloid' knocked in her head against other words like it – 'cellophane', 'cellular', 'celanese'. Now she did not know which she was

21

made of, but any of them seemed to describe her well.

'I like you to be made of celluloid,' said Mr Plantaganet quickly, as if he were afraid that what Tottie said might hurt Birdie, but Birdie did not mind.

'Marchpane was made of kid and china,' said Tottie.

'Kid? What is kid?'

'It is a kind of leather, white leather,' said Tottie. 'Her body was made of it and stuffed with sawdust and jointed; her joints worked more smoothly than mine. Her head was china, and her eyes were china too. Her hair was real, in a plait that they pinned round her head. You could plait it and unplait it.'

'Was it yellow?' asked Birdie.

'Yes,' said Tottie mournfully.

'Is there – much – difference between real and unreal? I wouldn't know,' said Birdie.

'Well – ye-es,' said Tottie as gently as she could.

'Did her clothes take on and off?' asked Apple, who hated to have his clothes taken off.

'She was in wedding clothes,' said Tottie. 'They took off and they were all white.'

'White? I shouldn't like that,' said Birdie more

22

cheerfully. 'I like pink and red and yellow and blue.'

'But they were beautiful. They were stitched with tiny featherstitching.'

'Is there a stitch called featherstitching? Oh, I should like that!' said Birdie, forgetting Marchpane.

'And they were edged with narrowest real lace.'

'Prr-ickkk!' said Darner suddenly. They looked at him in surprise. They all looked round for the danger and could not see any.

'Were those curtains real lace curtains?' asked Mr Plantaganet. 'Those curtains in the house?'

'I shouldn't suppose so,' said Tottie. 'Real lace is very expensive.'

'If it were my house,' said Mr Plantaganet, 'I should have real lace curtains. Nothing less,' said Mr Plantaganet firmly. 'Think! To live in a house like that.' His eyes, that Emily now kept quite free from dust, shone (being glass, they shone quite easily). 'Not to live in a shoe-box any more.' His voice changed as he said that; he sounded as if he were shut in the dark toy cupboard again.

'I could get out of my cot,' said Apple suddenly.

'I would. I could climb through the bars and Emily and Charlotte would think I had rolled out.'

Birdie was thinking about the bird, her songs, her hat, its feather, featherstitching, the feather broom.

'And when they had finished playing with us,' said Mr Plantaganet, 'they would shut up the front and we should be alone, quite private in our own house.'

'Yes,' said Tottie. 'I had forgotten how good that can be.'

She had forgotten Marchpane as well.

# Chapter 3

It was late autumn.

How do dolls know when it is autumn? The same way that you do. They smell the London autumn smells of bonfires, of newly lit chimneys, of fog and leaves soaking in the wet. When they go out they see that Michaelmas daisies are out in the Park and chrysanthemums are in the flower shops and violets have come back on to the street flower-sellers' trays. The grownups talk of the first winter colds, and winter coats, and the difficulties of central heating, and the children begin to think of parties and dancing class and even Christmas.

It was also, of course, much colder. It was cold in the shoe-boxes in the colder weather; their cardboard sides were thin and too low to keep out draughts, and Mr Plantaganet began to suffer. He was delicate little doll and he looked quite drawn with cold. Emily was knitting Tottie a cloak in red wool. 'I do wish she were knitting a muffler or a little waistcoat for Mr Plantaganet instead,' said Tottie. She could go no further than wishing. Dolls cannot tell anything, but often their wishing is as strong as telling. Have you never felt a doll's wish? I am afraid Emily did not feel Tottie's; she finished the cloak and tried it on and Tottie looked very well in it. Mr Plantaganet remained cold, a little miserable, a little neglected, and draughty in the shoe-box.

Then it happened, in that very autumn, that Emily and Charlotte's great-aunt died, the very great-aunt who had been the little girl of that Great-Great-Aunt Laura who had owned the dolls' house and gathered the shells at the seaside. Her relations and friends found a dolls' house in the attic, an old dolls' house on which the cream paint was dirtied and hung with cobwebs, but on which painted ivy could be seen. It had a green front door with a knocker and six steps going up to it, exactly as Tottie had described.

'Fancy this being here,' said the friends and relations.

'What shall we do with it?'

'It could be sold,' they said. 'It is really as good as new.'

This was not quite true, for it was dusty and thick with dirt; the butler had gone quite to dust, the velvet of the sofa and chairs was rotten and ripped, the shells had come off the pictures in places, and the lace curtains were torn.

'Still, it would fetch a good price,' they said.

'I don't think it ought to be sold,' said one relation who perhaps had more heart than the others. 'It was played with by Great-Aunt, perhaps by her mother. Are there no little girls in the family who might like to play with it now?'

There were two little girls. There were Emily and Charlotte.

The letter came at breakfast when the Plantaganet family were on the hearthrug where Charlotte had arranged them, pretending it was a park. When Mother read the letter they listened with all their ears, except Apple, whom Charlotte had incautiously put to play up on the fire irons. He was sliding dangerously near the dirty coals. Tottie was watching him from the corner of her eye.

'Can we have it, Mother?' begged Emily and Charlotte.

'Oh, can we?'

'Can we?' begged the Plantaganet family, except Apple.

'You had better ask Father.'

'Can we, Father?'

'Can we?'

'Can we?'

'Can we?' begged the Plantaganets.

Apple was getting nearer and nearer to the coal.

'We had better take it,' said Father. 'And then we can advertise it in the newspapers and get twenty-five pounds.'

'Do we need twenty-five pounds?' asked Mr Plantaganet, but Tottie told him Father was only teasing.

'I wish he wouldn't only tease,' said Mr Plantaganet. Mr Plantaganet could never tell when Father was teasing. 'Ought Fathers to tease?' he asked wistfully. 'Perhaps I am not a proper sort of Father.' He very much wanted to be a proper sort of everything. 'A house!' said Mr Plantaganet, forgetting Father. 'I suppose it is that house, Tottie?'

'I should think it must be,' said Tottie in her calming, calm wood voice. 'An old dolls' house that belonged to Great-Great-Aunt Laura. What else could it be?'

'That – that dream house?' said Mr Plantaganet.

'You didn't dream it, I told you of it,' said Tottie, who was strictly truthful; she could see Mr Plantaganet was getting into a state.

'I can't believe it,' said Mr Plantaganet. 'I can't. '

'Yes, you can,' said Tottie, 'easily. Now Father has said "Yes," it is going to happen.'

'No more shoe-boxes!' said Mr Plantaganet, with a catch in his voice. 'And it has been awfully cold in those shoe-boxes sometimes, hasn't it, Tottie?'

'Yes, but that's all over now,' said Tottie. 'At least, soon it will be over. Apple! Apple! Take care!'

'That little doll is nearly in the coal,' said Father, and he touched Apple with his foot.

Charlotte picked him out of the fender just in time.

'And Birdie will have her birdcage, and Apple will have his cot, and Darner his kennel.'

'And you will be able to wish Emily and Charlotte to shut the front when they have done playing with us, and I am sure they will,' said Tottie. 'And we shall live there happy ever after.'

'Yes. Oh yes! Oh YES!' said Mr Plantaganet, and he said to himself, 'No more shoe-boxes. No more dark toy cupboards. No more dark at all; we shall have the little lamp and even if they forget the candle, with a lamp it is easy to pretend that it is light. Red walls,' whispered Mr Plantaganet, 'taps that really run (if you fill the tank first), wax roses in the vase, nicked blankets on the beds.'

His eyes looked as if they might break their glass. No doll can cry tears, they have to keep their tears in, but Mr Plantaganet's eyes looked as if they held tears of joy. Did you know people could cry for joy as well as for sorrow? They can, and dolls would too sometimes if they could.

'Happy ever after,' said Mr Plantaganet. 'Happy ever after, Tottie.'

As I told you, they had forgotten Marchpane.

# Chapter 4

When the dolls' house arrived, Marchpane was not in it.

She had been sent to the cleaners.

That was very bad for Marchpane. The cleaners took such care of her that it went to her head which, being china, was empty, which is a very dangerous kind of head to have. Mr Plantaganet had one too, and it had been filled with his gloomy thoughts of dark toy cupboards and boys who drew moustaches, but now it was more happily filled with thoughts of the dolls' house. Marchpane's was filled with thoughts of Marchpane; and at the cleaners she thought how wonderful Marchpane was: how valuable Marchpane was: how beautifully Marchpane was made: what elegant clothes Marchpane had, with what small exquisite stitching. 'I am a beautiful little creature, really I am,' thought Marchpane. 'I must be worth a fabulous amount of money. No wonder they are so careful of me. They can hardly be careful enough. I am so very important,' said Marchpane. There was no one to contradict her and her thoughts of Marchpane grew larger and larger till you would have thought her little head was hardly big enough to contain them.

The cleaners took off her fine-sewn wedding clothes and washed and cleaned them exquisitely so that they were whiter than snowdrops or snow. Then they cleaned Marchpane herself all over and she was whiter too, but they cleaned her with petrol, and after it, I must confess, she smelled strongly and nastily of petrol: in fact, ever afterwards, she had a faintly nasty smell (which was quite right, because she was nasty).

The cleaners redressed her, and replaited her hair, which they had cleaned until it looked like golden floss; then, having politely asked permission first, they put her on the counter of their shop, with a card:

*Mid-nineteenth-century doll, as cleaned by us.*

Marchpane stood on the counter and everyone who came into the shop looked at her and admired her. Marchpane liked being looked at and admired more and more, though she thought of course it was only her due, and that the people were very lucky to have a chance to see such an elegant and beauteous doll as Marchpane.

# Chapter 5

Charlotte and Emily, the Plantaganet family, had been busy.

The dolls' house was exactly as Tottie had described it, but . . .

'Oh dear!' said Mr Plantaganet, and if the corners of his mouth had been made to turn down, they would have turned down.

'Oh dear! Oh dear! O-oh dear!'

On the dolls' house, and in it, were years and years of dust and grime and cobwebs and mold and rust. The children and the Plantaganets looked at the tattered chair and sofa covers, at the torn old curtains, at the sea-shells fallen off the picture frames, at the remains of the butler. The blue tin stove was rusty and so was the bath, the mangle was stuck, some of the kitchen chairs were broken and the nicked-round blankets were grey with mildew. 'Oh dear! Oh dear!' said Mr Plantaganet.

'Stop staying "Oh dear!"' said Tottie sharply.

'But what shall we do? What can we do?'

'We can wish,' said Tottie still sharply because, truth to tell, she was feeling worried and anxious herself. Could the children, would the children, be able to put it in order? That was the question in Tottie's mind.

'It's dusty. It's dirty. It's horrible!' cried little Apple.

'Is it?' asked Birdie anxiously. She could not herself see anything more than the birdcage and the bird. They were so wonderful to Birdie that she could not see anything else, and, being two things of the same kind, she did not feel the thoughts of them knocking together in her head.

'Is it dusty and dirty, Tottie?' asked Birdie.

'Wish! Wish! Wish!' said Tottie, and every knot

and grain of her seemed to harden. She came from a tree.

'What shall we do? What can we?' said Mr Plantaganet.

'Don't bleat. Wish,' said Tottie hardly, and her hard voice made the word sound so hard and firm that even Mr Plantaganet took heart and they all began to wish. 'Wish that Emily and Charlotte can put our house in order and make it good again. Go on, all of you. Wish. Wish. Wish,' said Tottie.

At that moment, among the Plantaganets appeared hands, Emily and Charlotte's hands, lifting them on to the mantelpiece out of the way where they could see. Then those same hands began to strip the dolls' house.

'What did I tell you?' said Tottie.

'But – they are not making it, they are taking it all away.'

'Taking it all to pieces.'

'Taking it all away.'

'Wait and see,' said Tottie. 'Wait and see.'

Emily and Charlotte and their mother took everything out of the dolls' house; they took the carpets up from their tintacks and with the carpets came layers of dust. They did not look like carpets but pieces of crinkled old grey flannel. Birdie hid her face in her hands. 'I wanted the pink one and there isn't a pink one,' she said.

'Wait and see. Wait and see,' said Tottie.

'The carpets are filthy,' said Mother. 'I will take them to wash and iron.'

'What did I say?' said Tottie.

Meanwhile Charlotte was brushing down the walls and roof, Emily was brushing out the rooms and stairs. Then Charlotte fetched a pail of water and a cake of soap and her nail brush.

'Charlotte, do you think you ought to use that?'

'Hush!' said Charlotte, beginning to use it. She washed the walls and roof and Emily, after watching a moment, joined in and, fetching her nail brush, began to wash the floor and walls and ceilings. She was a little astonished because she was the one who usually thought of things; it was unusual for Charlotte to be the first. 'H'm,' said Emily, scrubbing hard. 'Charlotte must like the dolls' house very very much.' The grime was so deep, the dust so thick, that they had to change the water in the pail three times.

'London grime,' said Tottie, watching. 'A hundred years of London grime.'

'I hope she doesn't miss the front steps,' said Mr Plantaganet, but Charlotte did not miss the front steps. She missed nothing at all. By the time she had finished she herself was filthy, with a filthy overall and dirt marks on her cheeks. Then she took a dry cloth and dried the walls and roof and steps all over; then took a duster and polished them. Emily watched again and followed her.

'Good work, Charlotte,' she said.

'Yes, good work,' said Tottie.

'Good work,' cried all the Plantaganets.

'Why, it begins to look new,' said Emily, stepping back from the dolls' house.

Indeed it looked much better. The good paint, and paint was good in those days, had come up well, and the wallpapers, from their brushing, had lost their look of grime. Charlotte had knocked down a few more shells from the pictures, but Emily had fetched the glue and glued them on again, which was unusual for Emily because she did not usually do things for Charlotte. She also brushed and dusted the furniture and rubbed the rust off the stove with sandpaper; she pulled the curtains down from the windows to which they had been fastened with drawing-pins and ripped the covers off the sofa and the chairs. Soon beds, chairs, and windows were left quite bare.

'Are you still wishing, Tottie?' asked Mr Plantaganet anxiously.

'Yes,' said Tottie firmly.

'You – see what I mean, don't you?' said Mr Plantaganet.

'You must wish about the curtains,' said Tottie. 'You must wish about the couch and chairs. You must wish about the beds.'

'Curtains, chairs, beds,' said Mr Plantaganet. He wished he could shut his eyes in order to wish harder but, of course, he could not because they were not made to shut.

'Over and over again,' said Tottie. 'You must never leave off wishing.'

'Beds, chairs, couch, curtains; beds, chairs, couch, curtains; beds, chairs . . . '

'My cot. My own little cot,' wished Apple.

'My bird-broom-feather.' Birdie still did not know which to think of first.

'Beds, couch, curtains, chairs . . . '

The door opened and the children's mother came in.

'Could she have washed those carpets already?' asked Mr Plantaganet suspiciously.

She answered him herself. 'I have washed the carpets,' said Mother. 'They have come up beautifully. Now I have brought the scrap bag; we shall need new mattresses and pillows and sheets and blankets for the beds.'

'And pillow cases,' said Charlotte, 'for mouse-size pillows.'

Emily stared at Charlotte, and so did the Plantaganets. It was not usually Charlotte who said things.

'Could I have a mouse-size pillow?' asked Apple, excited. 'A pillow for a very small mouse?'

'I shall fetch the cotton wool,' said Emily, 'and then I can stuff them as you make them.'

'But – but – I don't want cotton for mine,' cried Birdie, 'I want – want – want –' Her head rattled so that she could not say what it was she wanted. Tottie began to wish.

'I think Birdie ought to have a feather bed,' said Charlotte suddenly.

'A-aah!' said Birdie rapturously.

'Here are some bits of flannel for blankets. We can nick them round the edges,' said Mother. 'And what do you think? Shall we make Apple a patch-work quilt for his cot?'

'Could you make the patches small enough?' asked Emily. Mother thought she could.

'It is getting better and better and better,' said Mr Plantaganet.

'Yes!' said Birdie.

'Yes, but you must go on wishing,' said Tottie. 'You mustn't leave off wishing.'

'While I am in this cleaning mood,' said Charlotte, 'I am going to wash the windows. What shall we do about curtains?' asked Charlotte.

'They should be lace,' said Mother.

Then Emily spoke. 'They must be real lace,' said Emily.

Mr Plantaganet smiled.

'Real lace is very expensive,' said Mother.

'I shall get my money box,' answered Emily.

'Get mine too,' said Charlotte.

'What is the difference between real lace and not-real lace?' whispered Birdie.

'It is made by hand and not by machine,' said Tottie slowly, 'and it shows the care that was taken to make it, and besides being fine, it is strong, every least bit of it, and it looks different and it feels different. You would know the difference if you saw the two together.'

'Do you think I would?' asked Birdie humbly. 'Real things and not-real things, they seem the same to me. My bird and its songs –' She knew one was real and one was not, but she could not say now which was which.

Emily came back with the money boxes. They were rather empty; hers had a threepenny bit, a half-crown and a florin and a sixpenny bit in it. 'Five shillings and threepence,' said Emily. Charlotte's had a florin, sixpence, four three-penny bits, and a penny. 'Three shillings and sevenpence,' said Emily, 'eight and tenpence altogether. That might be enough but – there are other things we want as well,' said Emily. There was a gleam in her eyes as she looked at the old couch and chairs.

'I shall measure the windows,' said Charlotte and she measured them with Mother's tape measure. They were six inches long. 'Six inches, and there are four windows. Four times six is twenty-four, twenty-four inches, and twenty-seven inches is three-quarters of a yard. We should have to buy three-quarters of a yard of that real lace,' said

Charlotte. 'And we should have three inches over. We could make a lace apron for Tottie.'

'Yes, but we need a new couch and chairs.'

The couch and chairs, now they were stripped, certainly looked in very bad repair; their wooden arms and legs were scratched and stained and they had no stuffing left on their seats and backs at all.

'Not a little patch of that red velvet,' said Mr Plantaganet.

'There are others in the shops,' said Charlotte uncertainly.

'Yes, ordinary ones,' said Emily scornfully.

'Wouldn't – wouldn't ordinary ones do?' Charlotte was a little like Birdie. She was happy with ordinary things, but Emily was not.

'This dolls' house is special,' said Emily. 'You know it is, Charlotte. It is an antique,' said Emily.

'What is an an— what she said then?' asked Mr Plantaganet.

'Yes, what is it?'

'What is it, Tottie?'

'Old things are antiques,' said Tottie. 'Things that have lasted for many years, usually because they were beautifully made of good materials in the beginning.'

'Like real lace,' said Mr Plantaganet.

'Yes, and usually they have been given great care or they would not have lasted all that time,' said Tottie.

'Like the dolls' house?' asked Birdie. 'It is an antique. Emily said so.'

'Are you an antique, Tottie?' asked Apple suddenly.

'I suppose I am,' said Tottie.

'I know what would look very beautiful on that holly-green carpet,' Emily was saying slowly. 'Do you know, Charlotte?'

'What?' asked Charlotte.

'Do you remember looking at that shop in Wigmore Street?' said Emily, 'where they had that little set of dolls' house chairs and couch? They were very old and they were made of real oak – it said so – and they were red velvet too.'

'And there was a table,' said Charlotte dreamily, 'and it had a red runner and a fringe.'

'Yes,' said Emily.

'Yes,' said Charlotte.

'Yes,' said the Plantaganets.

'I shall have sixpence for my tooth when it comes out,' said Charlotte.

'Oh, Charlotte! Don't be silly,' said Emily. 'Those were terribly expensive.'

'Then – we shall have to have ordinary lace and chairs.'

'Oh no!' cried Mr Plantaganet. 'Oh no! Please no!'

'I don't mind ordinary chairs,' said Birdie. 'I can make do with anything.'

'We can't,' said Emily. 'We shan't.'

'But – what shall we do?'

'We shall do what other people do when they want things,' said Emily. 'We must make money.'

'But how?' asked Charlotte.

'How?' asked all the Plantaganets.

'Somehow,' said Emily.

# Chapter 6

Tottie and the dolls' house were not the only things in the house that had belonged to Emily and Charlotte's great-grandmother and Great-Great-Aunt Laura. There was, as well, a sampler.

'What is a sampler?' asked Apple.

'It is a needlework picture to hang on a wall,' Tottie explained to him. 'It is all worked in cross-stitch on fine canvas, and sometimes, most times, the stitches are very fine indeed. Do you remember, in *The Tailor of Gloucester*,' asked Tottie, 'when it says, "the stitches were so small – *so* small, that they could only have been made by mice'? Well, the stitches in samplers look like that, but they were not made by mice,' said Tottie. 'They were made by little girls; and hours and hours of stitching went into them. They had letters and alphabets and a great deal of writing. I remember them well,' said Tottie. 'I feel glad that little girls do not have to make them now,' said Tottie.

Great-Grandmother's sampler hung in the children's room. It was long in shape and framed in a narrow wooden frame. It was worked in baskets of flowers on a cream background, and it had a verse that said in tiny pale-blue stitches:

> *Fain am I to work these nosegays*
> *Gathered from my tranquil days*
> *In gentle rain, mild storm and sunny weather,*
> *A friend to flower, flesh and fur and feather,*
> *Content, please God, my time on earth to dwell*
> *Till death shall claim me and I say farewell.*

'I remember those *f*'s,' said Tottie. 'They gave her a great deal of trouble.'

Charlotte did not like to look at the sampler, she said it gave her a headache and she did not understand the poem in the least, but Emily liked it. Sometimes she begged Mother to give her a certain little set of clothes, Tottie's first clothes, as old as the sampler. These clothes were not beautiful ones like Marchpane's; they were the ordinary clothes that might have been made for any little doll in those times: a bodice with infinitesimal tucks where stay-bones should have been, a pair of long-legged drawers scalloped to match, and a dress of India muslin embroidered in blue flowers, and a very little blue bonnet to mach that had white embroidery that looked like quilling on the edge. Emily liked to dress Tottie in these and stand her underneath the sampler.

'Let's put her there today, Charlotte,' said Emily next afternoon. 'Mrs Innisfree is coming to tea.'

Both the children loved Mrs Innisfree, who was gay and serious as need arose and who was always interested in their dolls. Emily dressed Tottie and stood her under the sampler and even wrote a ticket that said, not unlike the cleaners' notice for Marchpane: *Example of a real old sampler worked by a little girl in 1846.*

'Poor little girl,' said Charlotte indignantly.

Emily took no notice. She wrote: *Example of a far-thing doll, dressed by that same little girl in 1846.*

'Her mother must have helped her,' said Charlotte. 'No little girl could make that quilling. You ought to put in about the mother, Emily.'

'Well, I shan't,' said Emily. 'It spoils the notice.'

There was a sound of footsteps outside the door and Mrs Innisfree came in. She admired Tottie and the sampler and she admired the dolls' house, and she sat down by the fire and listened to the whole story of it.

'It's a pity about the chairs and couch,' said Mrs Innisfree.

Emily told her about the set in Wigmore Street, and then she and Charlotte fell silent.

'They sound the very thing,' said Mrs Innisfree. 'Will you buy them?'

'No-o,' said Emily.

'No-o,' said Charlotte.

'At least, not yet,' said Emily with a faraway brightness in her eyes.

'I see,' said Mrs Innisfree, and her eyes went to Tottie. 'It is strange,' she said, 'that you should have arranged Tottie like that for me to see. I am having an exhibition,' said Mrs Innisfree, 'at least a part of it is mine. It is called "Dolls Through the Ages", and it is to help the Blind Children's Fund. I wonder if your little doll and sampler could be in it.'

'You mean, just as they are now?' asked Charlotte. '*"Example of a real old sampler worked by a little girl in 1846"* (poor little girl), and *"Example of a farthing doll dressed by that same little girl in 1846"* (only you ought to have put in about the mother doing the quilling),' said Charlotte.

'Yes, I mean that,' said Mrs Innisfree. 'I think your mother would let you, and,' said Mrs Innisfree, looking at Emily and Charlotte and at the shabby little chairs and empty windows of the dolls' house, 'we pay for some of the dolls, and I should like to pay you for Tottie.'

When Tottie heard these words she gave a little gasp, but no one heard her.

'How much would you pay?' Charlotte was saying. 'Would you pay a whole pound?'

'Charlotte!' said Emily and tried to kick her gently on the ankle.

'But we need a whole pound,' said Charlotte.

'We should pay a guinea,' said Mrs Innisfree.

Tottie gave another sound and this time it was a groan, but Apple was tugging at her skirt.

'How much is a guinea?' whispered Apple.

'A pound and a shilling,' said Tottie faintly. 'Mrs Innisfree is giving that for me. O-oh! Oh!'

'That would be enough,' said Charlotte, nodding her head.

'After a hundred years!' cried Tottie.

'Then will you let me take Tottie and the sampler away?' asked Mrs Innisfree.

'Take Tottie away –' cried Mr Plantaganet, and stopped.

'Tottie? Going away?' asked Birdie.

'Tottie go away?' asked little Apple, and he said firmly, 'No.'

'Now, Apple –'

'No! No! No!' cried Apple.

'It is to get the chairs,' said Mr Plantaganet.

'Don't want any chairs.'

'Now, Apple!'

'I don't want any either. Bother the chairs,' said Birdie. 'Can't we sit on cotton reels? They would do.'

'We have to have elegant chairs,' said Mr Plantaganet slowly. 'Here is a good way of Tottie earning them. Isn't it like Tottie,' asked Mr Plantaganet, 'to be the one to earn us a couch and chairs, and the table with the runner, and the real lace curtains perhaps as well?'

Tottie said nothing at all. She stood as if, instead of being wood, she had turned to stone, and when Emily picked her up and wrapped her in white paper to give to Mrs Innisfree, Tottie lay cold and heavy in her hand. Emily felt misery and reproach from Tottie, but she did not understand why. Can you guess why?

Tottie was wrapped up and packed in a box, the box laid on top of the sampler with the two notices, and they were all handed to Mrs Innisfree.

# Chapter 7

In the night Apple would not sleep without Tottie, Birdie had no wish to sleep, and even Mr Plantaganet did not feel quite comfortable.

'Go to sleep, Apple, do,' he said.

'You go to sleep,' said Apple.

But Mr Plantaganet could not. Emily and Charlotte were strangely restless too.

'Emily,' said Charlotte at last from her bed.

'Yes, Charlotte.'

'You will be cross,' said Charlotte.

'I don't think I will,' said Emily. 'I-I think I know what you are thinking, Charlotte.'

'Well,' said Charlotte, and she lay on her back looking thoughtfully up at the ceiling. 'Well, people usually do, don't they?'

'Do what?'

'Lend, not be paid,' said Charlotte.

'Ye-es,' said Emily miserably.

'I mean, for an exhibition like that, which is to help people, people usually lend their things, don't they, to help the other people?'

'That's what I was thinking-remembering,' said Emily. 'Do you remember the animal carving exhibition we went to see? It had labels: *Head of a deer, lent by Mr So-and-So. Rabbit, lent by Mrs Somebody Else.*'

'Ye-es,' said Charlotte.

'It didn't say, *Hired from Mr So-and-So,*' said Emily, 'and that is what being paid means. We have hired out Tottie.'

'That is what she didn't like,' said Charlotte, and she was near the truth though that was not the whole truth.

'I felt her being miserable, but I didn't take any notice – then,' said Emily.

'Nor I,' said Charlotte. 'But I wish I had.'

'I believe Mrs Innisfree offered to pay us because she was sorry we couldn't get the chairs,' said Emily.

'We shall go to Mrs Innisfree in the morning and tell her,' said Emily. 'I believe she knew we really ought not to have been paid.'

'I believe we really knew that too,' said Charlotte. 'It was my fault,' she added. 'I said we needed a pound.'

'No, it was mine,' said Emily. 'I wanted the chairs more than you did. How funny. I want things so hard, Charlotte, that I don't think what I am doing. I don't want them so much now,' said Emily.

'Then we shall have ordinary ones?' asked Charlotte.

'No,' said Emily firmly and shortly.

'Then what will you do?'

'I don't know what I shall do,' said Emily, 'but not this,' she said.

Mrs Innisfree was surprised to see them when they called at her house next morning. She seemed more surprised and pleased when Emily laid the pound note and the shilling on the table.

'After all,' said Charlotte, 'we are not blind and

if we don't get paid for Tottie, the children who are blind will get more money.'

'Certainly they will,' said Mrs Innisfree, and she looked at Emily, who had put down the pound note and the shilling and who could not trust herself to speak.

'Emily,' said Mrs Innisfree, 'you wanted those chairs badly, didn't you?'

'Yes,' said Emily, 'but Charlotte likes the dolls' house just as much as I do.'

'It was your idea to get those chairs?'

'And the couch and the table and the runner,' put in Charlotte.

'Well – I saw them first,' said Emily.

'Emilys usually see things first,' said Mrs Innisfree gently. 'And it is usually they who have the ideas. I am like Emily; it was my idea to pay you for Tottie, but of course it is far nicer that you yourselves have decided to lend her to me. Now I have another idea,' said Mrs Innisfree.

(You must remember that while this was happening Tottie was packed away in her box under her paper and had no idea of it at all. You must keep remembering that.)

'I want,' said Mrs Innisfree, 'to see those old

chairs and that old couch. The ones that were in the dolls' house when it came.'

'But – they are all torn and unstuffed.'

'But the wooden part, the legs and arms and frames?'

'That is still there,' said Charlotte.

'They should be as good as new, if they were as good in the first place as I think they were. As good as the Wigmore Street ones,' said Mrs Innisfree. 'Go and get them now,' she said.

'What now? Straight away?' asked Charlotte, but Emily's eyes gleamed.

'Straight away,' said Mrs Innisfree. 'I might be able to do something with them if they are as I hope.'

'Are they?' asked Charlotte an hour later when she and Emily had come back.

'Are they what?'

'As you hoped?'

'Yes, they are,' said Mrs Innisfree.

The sofa and chairs stood on the table in her drawing room. 'Look,' she said, and with her scissors she ripped off what Emily had left of the stuffing, the torn bits, and dirty old cotton; soon the chairs and sofa were bare down to their seats.

'Look,' said Mrs Innisfree, 'the wood is good, quite solid. Do you see, Emily, the little legs are turned. They are scratched and discoloured, but the good work is there. Do you see that when things are beautifully made, how beautifully they last?'

'These don't look as if they had lasted,' objected Charlotte. 'They look fit to throw away.'

'That is because you haven't looked into them. Wait and see,' said Mrs Innisfree. She opened a drawer and took out two pieces of sandpaper and rubbed them against each other. 'That's to smooth them a little because they are too rough – they must not scratch the wood too deeply.' She picked up a little chair and began to rub its leg.

'But – you are taking all its polish off.'

'And the dirt and scratches. Now you and Charlotte rub them, and when they are quite clean and smooth we shall take them to a man I know who is a French polisher, and we shall ask him if he will help us. I think he will,' said Mrs Innisfree.

'But – would a real French polisher polish them?'

'He might, if we can make him interested,' said Mrs Innisfree. 'People will do anything if they are interested.'

'But what about the seats and arms and backs? They were all cushioned before.'

'They can be cushioned again.'

'But with what? Mother says that nowhere, anymore, anywhere, can you buy stuff like that they were cushioned with,' said Emily.

'Have you seen this?' asked Mrs Innisfree, and she picked up a footstool that was standing by the table and showed it to them. Its top was of embroidery, flowers, worked very finely, in the same mice stitches that Tottie had talked about, stitches like the sampler, only finer.

'This is called *petit-point*. Have you ever seen a chair like it?' asked Mrs Innisfree. 'A tapestry chair?'

'Oh!' said Emily. 'Oh! You mean—'

'Yes. What could be better than tiny tapestry chairs and couch?' asked Mrs Innisfree.

'Dolls' tapestry would have to be very, very fine,' said Emily slowly. 'Could anybody work it?' she asked doubtfully.

'I have worked it so that it was very fine indeed.'

'It would be beautiful,' breathed Charlotte. 'But we couldn't do it, not Emily, nor I. It would take us years and years to learn. Our great-grandmother could have done it. Perhaps there was some use in working samplers,' said Charlotte mournfully. 'Now who – who – who –'

Mrs Innisfree had not answered. She had opened a drawer and was taking out a roll of fine canvas and a box of silks.

'You!' said Emily and Charlotte together. 'You! You mean you would work it for us?'

'It would not take me very long,' said Mrs Innisfree. 'I think I could do it. Anyway, I could try. Suppose you stay to lunch with me and then we could choose patterns and colours. Of course we shall need an upholsterer as well as a French polisher,' said Mrs Innisfree, 'but I have another friend who would do that for us. I think it will be far nicer and of course far cheaper,' she said with a sideways look at the children, 'than the little set in Wigmore Street that you wanted to buy.'

'What a great deal we are learning about things,' said Emily, 'all these beautiful old things.'

'But you mustn't think it is only the old things that are beautiful,' said Mrs Innisfree. 'We can do as good work nowadays if we have the same patience.'

'Yes – patience!' said Charlotte. Truth to tell, her

hand was aching very much from the sandpapering, but she went on rubbing.

They had lunch with Mrs Innisfree. What did they have? They had plaice, which is fish, and green peas and mashed potatoes, and a cherry tart from Mrs Innisfree's bottled cherries.

After lunch they looked through the patterns and silk and chose a small pattern that was part of a larger pattern; it was moss rosebuds in crimson and pink, with green leaves, on a cream background. 'And we must have this copper colour for the stems,' said Mrs Innisfree, 'and I shall use this peacock blue for the shading.'

'Can you shade so tiny?' asked Emily.

'I think I can,' said Mrs Innisfree.

'I think you can do anything,' said Charlotte, and that evening she said to Emily, 'Do you know, Emily, Mrs Innisfree reminds me of Tottie.'

'Of Tottie?'

'Yes.'

'Can a real person remind you of a doll?'

'I don't know,' said Charlotte, 'but Mrs Innisfree does.' She thought for a moment. 'Perhaps it's because Tottie never breaks or gets spoilt. I miss Tottie,' said Charlotte.

They had asked to peep at Tottie before they left Mrs Innisfree, and how surprised Tottie was to see their faces bending over her.

'Is this all a bad dream?' asked Tottie of herself. 'Am I at home again?' But as soon as Charlotte lifted her up she saw that she was in a strange room and that the box still lay on the table. 'It isn't a dream,' cried Tottie in Charlotte's hand. 'Oh! Oh! Oh!'

'Why does she look so unhappy?' asked Charlotte.

'A pound and a shilling! A guinea. After a hundred years,' said Tottie.

'She looks – angry,' said Emily. Both of them could feel Tottie wishing, but they could not understand why she should wish, and they put her back into the box and covered her up with tissue paper.

'When does she go to the Exhibition?' she heard Emily ask, just before they put on the lid.

'To the Exhibition! To the Exhibition!' said Tottie in a cry so loud that every knot and grain of her felt twisted, but, of course, not a sound came out of the box.

# Chapter 8

Marchpane had been seen by someone at the cleaners who had taken her address and written to the great-aunt's relations to ask if Marchpane too might not come to the Exhibition.

The great-aunt's relations said yes.

Marchpane was delighted.

# Chapter 9

When Tottie was next taken out of her box she found herself in a large cold room that had long tables, covered with blue cloth, against each wall, and a number of ladies all busy unpacking dolls.

Tottie had never seen so many ladies and so many dolls, particularly so many dolls. There was every kind of doll: baby dolls, little girl dolls, boy dolls, lady and gentleman dolls, soldier dolls, sailor dolls, acting dolls, dancing dolls, clockwork dolls, fairy dolls, Chinese dolls, Polish, Japanese,

French, German, Russian. There was a white wax doll with exquisite white china hands, and a Dutch fisherman with a basket on his back, and a Flemish doll in market clothes, and her cook sitting down with her basket. There were Japanese dolls with blank white faces, and Chinese dolls whose faces were as alive as snakes, with painted snaky eyebrows and long noses; they were dancers and ceremonial dolls with satin trousers and red-painted shoes. There were two little German dolls with yellow fringes and gentle brown eyes and peasant clothes, and a Polichinelle, very old, with his legs drawn up and a carved, frightening, evil face. There was every kind and sort of doll and they filled the room, each standing in its place and showing what kind of doll it was. Some of them were very handsome and imposing; all of them, without exception, were far, far larger than Tottie.

She felt small and shy and longed to go home. 'But I can't go home,' said Tottie. 'I shall never go home again,' and her secret trouble filled her so strongly that, if wood could have drooped, Tottie would have drooped. 'Oh! Oh! Oh!' cried poor little Tottie, and she thought of them all at home:

Mr Plantaganet, Birdie, Darner, Apple; when she thought of Apple she felt as if she must break into splinters, but of course, being made of such good wood, she gave no outward sign.

A lady took her up in her hand. 'Where shall we put this darling little thing?' she asked. 'Look. She goes with this sampler.'

'What a charming idea,' said another, but Tottie did not think it was in the least bit charming.

'A farthing doll!' said another lady. 'Why, I should think she must be unique.'

Tottie did not know what 'unique' meant (if you don't, go and look it up in the dictionary), for all she could tell it might be something rude, and she wished she could hang her head, but of course a wooden neck will never, never bend and so she stayed, staring as woodenly as possible, straight in front of her. The ladies took her and set her up on the centre of one of the long tables, with the sampler behind her and two square cards and one longer one in front of her. From Tottie's point of view, these cards were upside down, so that she could not read them. They looked like this:

FARTHING DOLL
DRESSED BY SAME
LITTLE GIRL OF 1846

SAMPLER WORKED
BY A LITTLE GIRL
IN 1846

LENT BY HER GREAT-GRANDDAUGHTERS,
EMILY AND CHARLOTTE DANE
in 1946

On the table opposite Tottie were four dolls under a glass-domed cover. Next to her, on her right side, was a wax doll with a satin dress, and on the other side a walking doll dressed in blue satin with a bustle behind and white flounces. She held, tiptilted, a blue parasol, and in the other tiny hand, a fan.

'Who – who are those in the case?' asked Tottie.

'They were Queen Victoria's dolls when she was a child,' said the wax doll.

'O-ooh!' said Tottie. She remembered Queen Victoria of course.

'La! We'ave been put in one of ze best positions, is it you say? in ze room,' said the walking doll.

'Why does she talk like that?' asked Tottie in a whisper of the wax doll.

'She is French,' said the wax doll. 'She is very proud.'

The walking doll held her tiptilted parasol and her fan and glanced at Tottie. 'What ees it you are made of?' she asked. '*Pardonnez-moi*, but la! I do not recognize ze substance.'

'I am made of wood,' answered Tottie with dignity.

'Wood? La! La! La! Tee-hee-hee.' Her laughing sounded as if it were wound up. 'Tee-hee. La! La! I thought doorknobs and broom 'andles and bedposts and clothes-pegs were made of wood, not dolls.'

'So they are,' said Tottie. 'And so are the masts of ships and flagpoles and violins – and trees,' said Tottie.

She and the walking doll looked at one another and, though the walking doll was quite ten inches taller than Tottie, Tottie did not flinch.

'I am made of keed and porcelain,' said the walking doll. 'Inside I 'ave a leetle set of works. Wind me up and I walk.'

'Walk, walk, walk,' cried the other dolls.

'*Merci! Je ne marcherai pas que si ça me chante*,' which means she would not walk unless she wanted, but of course she could not walk unless someone wound her up.

'I once knew a kid doll,' said Tottie. 'I did not like her.'

'Who is talking about kid dolls?' came a voice from the opposite table. 'Who did not like kid dolls?'

'I don't,' said Tottie firmly though, at the sound of that voice, she felt as if instead of being wood all through, she might have been made hollow inside.

'And who are you?' said the voice.

'It is a leetle object,' said the walking doll, 'that 'as found its way in 'ere. La! It is made of wood.'

'Of wood?' said the voice. 'Once I knew a little doll made of wood and I did not like her at all!'

'I 'ave nevaire see one,' said the walking doll.

'They were sold in the cheaper shops. A shilling a dozen or four for a penny. The children, silly little things, would waste their money on them.'

'La! Children! *Merci. Je ne mange pas de ce pain là.* 'Orrible leetle creatures. *Je les déteste.'*

'Silly little things! Little creatures! Those are children they are talking of!' said the wax doll, shocked. Her voice, after the others, was meltingly soft. 'How dare they!' said the wax doll. 'They don't deserve the name of "doll". But tell me about those things you were talking of – the ships and flagpoles.

It must be good to be made of something hard,' said the wax doll.

'It is,' said Tottie. At the moment all the good wood in her was standing firmly against the things the voice and the haughty doll had said. Tottie knew that voice. She looked across at the other table and she saw whom she had expected to see. She saw Marchpane. Marchpane saw her.

'Oh, it's you,' said Marchpane.

'Yes,' said Tottie.

'Strange!' said Marchpane. 'I thought you would have been broken or thrown away long, long ago.'

'No,' said Tottie.

'What is it they used to call you?' asked Marchpane. 'Spotty, Dotty. Surely it was Dotty.'

'Tee! Tee-hee! Tee-hee!' giggled the walking doll. 'Tee-hee-hee! Tee-hee!'

'My name is Tottie,' said Tottie. 'It always has been.'

'I couldn't be expected to remember,' said Marchpane. 'There were so many of you.'

'Not in our family,' said Tottie. 'I was the only one.'

'She is the only one now,' said the wax doll. 'The

only one of her kind in the Exhibition. I heard them say so.'

For some time there had been whispers going on among the dolls and now the walking doll was listening. 'La! Is it possible?' she asked. *'Non. Non. Je m'en doute.'*

'What is it?' asked Marchpane.

'Dey say that some of the dolls 'ere are to be sold, sold out of their families.'

'What? Sold by your own family?'

'Sold!'

'Sold!'

'Sold!' ran the whisper among the dolls.

*'La! Quel malheur!'* said the walking doll. 'My museum would nevaire part with me.'

'Nor mine,' said Marchpane quickly.

'Nor mine,' said the wax doll, but she said it with a fluttering sigh.

You notice that Tottie had said nothing all this time. This was Tottie's secret trouble. Yes, Tottie thought that Emily and Charlotte had sold her to Mrs Innisfree. If you look back to page 50 of this book you will see why. 'We pay for some of the dolls,' Mrs Innisfree had said. 'I should like to pay you for Tottie.'

'How much would you pay?' Charlotte had asked. Oh, Charlotte! 'Would you pay a whole pound?'

Tottie shuddered when she remembered that.

'We should pay a guinea,' said Mrs Innisfree.

Of course Tottie did not know that Emily and Charlotte had given the guinea back to Mrs Innisfree. She thought she was sold and would presently be sold again. She was filled with shame.

'It must be there on those cards,' thought Tottie. 'Only they can't read them because they are upside down and Marchpane is too far away on the other table. But soon they must know!' thought Tottie.

'La! I am glad I am not standing next to such a one,' said the walking doll.

'But you are. You are,' thought Tottie. She wished she could sink through the table.

The other dolls were longing for the Exhibition to open. Marchpane, of course, was eager for the people to come and admire her, and so was the haughty doll. The wax doll was excited. She had been packed away in a box so long. 'Do you think there will be any children?' she asked with longing in her voice.

'Children? I hope not!' said Marchpane.

'I 'ope zey will not touch,' said the haughty doll.

'They had better not touch me,' said Marchpane. 'That must certainly not be allowed.'

'But – were you not meant to be played with?' asked the wax doll. 'I was. I was.'

'La! You are un'appy?'

'I am shut away in a box. Away from children, and it is children who give us life,' said the wax doll.

'And tumble one about and spoil one,' said Marchpane, and the walking doll shuddered to the tip of her parasol.

'Isn't that life?' asked Tottie.

'I want children,' cried the wax doll. 'I-I –' She stopped. It had been on the tip of her tongue to say, 'I wish I could be sold.' She wished she dared to say this aloud, but wax is not very brave stuff and so she remained quiet.

Tottie wished the Exhibition would never open. 'But it will,' thought Tottie, 'and then – then – someone will buy me. I shall be sold and when the Exhibition closes I shall go away to a new home. Oh!' cried Tottie. 'Oh Apple! Darner! Birdie! Mr Plantaganet! My little home! Oh! Oh! Oh!' But no sign of grief showed on her wooden face. She stood as firm as ever.

'Is it true,' said one of the dolls, 'that this Exhibition is to be opened by a queen?'

'Queen Victoria?' asked the wax doll, looking at the dolls in the glass case. Tottie whispered to her that Queen Victoria had been dead long, long ago.

'Forgive me,' said the wax doll. 'I have been shut away so long.'

'A queen?' said Marchpane with great satisfaction. 'How right and proper. She will be sure to notice me. They always do,' she said, though Tottie was sure she had never seen a queen before. 'I am so glad I have been cleaned.'

'I always stay clean,' said Tottie. 'Wood can be washed and be none the worse.'

'So can scrubbing brushes,' said Marchpane tartly. 'I am afraid Her Majesty will have rather a disagreeable surprise,' said Marchpane. 'She can't have been told that there are farthing dolls in this Exhibition. Why, I don't suppose,' said Marchpane, opening her china-blue eyes wide, 'that she knows that such things exist.'

'Even queens can learn,' said Tottie quietly.

Every evening, when the Exhibition room was shut, a child came to look at the dolls.

'A child! A child! A child!' The whisper would

go through the room because so many of the dolls through being rare and precious had been for a long while put away in boxes or kept on shelves or in museums. They had not been near children for so long. They yearned toward this little girl who crept in to look at them. None of them yearned more than the wax doll.

The child was thin, with poor clothes, and she kept her hands behind her as if she had been told not to touch. She went from one doll to the other and stared with eyes that looked large in her thin face.

'La! You would think she 'ad nevaire see a doll before!' said the walking doll.

'Perhaps she hasn't, as close as this,' said Tottie. 'Dolls are scarce now and very expensive.'

'Quite right. They should never be given to children to be played with,' said Marchpane.

The wax doll looked at the child as if her heart would melt. 'Little darling!' she said. 'How good she is! How gentle! See, she doesn't even touch.'

At that moment the child took one hand from behind her back and stretched it out to the wax doll and, with a finger, very gently touched her satin dress. The wax doll trembled with pleasure from head to toe. After that the child came most often to look at the wax doll.

'I believe she is the caretaker's child,' said Marchpane.

'She is my child,' breathed the wax doll.

Now the day came for the Exhibition to be open. By eleven o'clock everything was dusted and ready; the ladies were waiting, the dolls were waiting, and a great number of other ladies and gentlemen and a few children, invited guests, were waiting. Marchpane and the haughty doll were preening their necks to hold them to the greatest advantage and setting off their dresses; the wax doll was looking at the children and thinking they were not as good as the caretaker's child; Tottie stood dreading and fearing the moment when someone would buy her and her secret must be told.

The Exhibition ladies kept coming along the tables and shifting and tidying what was arranged and neat already, and putting straight what was straight before.

'I do wish they wouldn't,' sighed Tottie.

'They are showing us every attention, naturally,' said Marchpane. 'We are very important – at least,' she corrected herself, 'some of us are.'

'I don't like attention,' said Tottie who had been dusted and flicked with a feather broom and stood up and down until she felt giddy.

There was a stir, a pause, the Queen had come. Presently they heard her voice. The Queen's voice was as clear, her words as distinct, as separate drops of water. *'Clear and cool, clear and cool.'* Tottie had heard that about water once, and the Queen's voice sounded to her like that.

'I have great pleasure in declaring this Exhibition open,' said the Queen's voice, and there was an immediate clapping of hands.

'Why are they clapping?' asked the wax doll.

'They are clapping us, of course,' said Marchpane.

'They are clapping the Queen,' said Tottie.

Now the ladies and gentlemen, following the Queen, who was attended by the ladies of the Exhibition and her own lady-in-waiting, began to come down the tables, looking at the dolls. The lady-in-waiting carried a bouquet of chrysanthemums. 'That is for us, I expect,' said Marchpane.

'How could it be for us? It's too big,' said Tottie, but by now Marchpane was so far gone in conceit that nothing looked big to her.

'But – she isn't wearing a crown!' said the wax doll, disappointed.

'She only wears a crown when she goes to Parliament and places like that,' said Tottie, who had learned about kings and queens when her little girls, from Great-Grandmother down to Charlotte, learned their history.

'She has the most elegant hat with grey feathers,' said Marchpane. 'I shall have one copied for myself. Shh. She is coming this way.'

'La! I am nairvous,' said the walking doll. *'Je ne me sens pas bien du tout,'* which means she did not feel well. The wax doll trembled, but the people thought it was their footsteps shaking the room. Tottie remained woodenly staring in front of her.

On the Queen came, stopping, looking, touching, this doll or that, asking questions. Then she stopped directly in front of Marchpane, as Marchpane had known she would.

'What a beautiful doll,' said the Queen. 'Surely she is the smallest in the Exhibition?'

Now in Marchpane's ears, the Queen could not have asked a more unfortunate question. Marchpane was not the smallest doll in the Exhibition. Tottie was, and Marchpane hated her for that. She almost cracked her china as she heard Mrs Innisfree say, 'There is one even smaller, Ma'am. This little farthing doll,' and saw the Queen turn away to Tottie.

'Oh!' said the Queen. 'Oh! I used to play with wooden dolls like this when I was a little girl.'

'A queen! With wooden dolls! How *very* surprising!' said the other dolls.

'*La! Comme c'est drôle!*' said the walking doll. As for Marchpane she said nothing. She was afraid she really would crack if she did.

'I haven't seen one for years and years,' said the Queen. 'My nurse used to buy them for me.' And then she asked the very question Tottie was dreading to hear. 'Is she for sale?' asked the Queen.

Every knot and grain in Tottie hardened as she waited for the answer to come. Whispers ran up and down the dolls.

'I should like to buy her if she is,' said the Queen.

'Birdie, Emily, Charlotte, Mr Plantaganet, Apple, Darner, Apple, goodbye,' whispered Tottie. She wished she could close her eyes to shut out the faces but, naturally, she had to keep them woodenly open. But – what was this that Mrs Innisfree was saying?

'I'm afraid not, Ma'am,' said Mrs Innisfree. 'She isn't for sale. She is the very dear possession of two little girls,' and she pointed to the card.

The Queen picked up the cards and read them out:

'"*Sampler, worked by a little girl in 1846.*" "*Farthing doll dressed by the same little girl in 1846.*" "*Lent by her great-granddaughters, Emily and Charlotte Dane, in 1946.*"'

'Of course,' said the Queen, 'she must be a great treasure. May I look at her?'

And Tottie was picked up in the pale grey glove of the Queen, who examined her and examined her clothes.

'Dear little thing,' said the Queen, and gave Tottie back to Mrs Innisfree and passed on down the tables.

'My dear, you 'ave 'ad a *succès fou!*' said the haughty doll. Tottie did not ask what a *succès fou* was. For the first time her wood felt weak, bending, and then one of the ladies ran forward with a cry. 'Oh dear!' she said, 'the little farthing doll has fallen over and rolled down right off the table.'

# Chapter 10

Tottie was not hurt.

Such happiness flowed through her that she felt as though the sap of her tree had risen in her wood, as it once had every spring, and was running through her.

'Tottie is happy because the Queen wanted to buy her,' said the other dolls.

'She is happy because the Queen couldn't buy her,' Tottie could have corrected them. 'But what was it all about?' asked Tottie. 'Emily and Charlotte must have had a change of heart.' That was as near as Tottie ever came to understanding the truth, and it was very near the truth.

'God bless the Queen,' said Tottie. 'God bless the Queen.'

But Marchpane was bitterly jealous.

# Chapter 11

Meanwhile the Plantaganet family had moved into the dolls' house.

They had made it completely their own. Though the chairs were not ready yet and the lace curtains had not come, Mr Plantaganet, Birdie, Apple, and Darner had settled down. The house was clean from top to bottom. There were new sheets and pillows, those mouse-size pillows, and nicked-round blankets on the beds. Apple had his patchwork quilt. The carpets were nailed down and their washing had made their colours fresh. 'Mine is pink, as pink as roses and apple blossom and nail polish,' sang Birdie. The rust had been scoured and scraped from the stove and pots and pans, and the sea-shells had been glued back again on the picture frames.

No family could have been happier than the Plantaganets were now. Darner had his kennel to himself, and it was filled with real chopped-up straw that Emily had begged from a stable in the mews and cut up with her scissors. Apple had the whole house to play in and he had learned the dangerous practice of somersaulting down the stairs. He wished that Charlotte would sit him at the top and then, quite soon, he would manage to overbalance and somersault down to the bottom. Birdie had her room with the pink carpet, and every morning she dusted it with her feather broom while she sang all the songs that she felt her bird in the birdcage would sing, though what of her was dusting and what singing, Birdie sometimes did not know.

'Do I sing with my hands and dust with my voice?' asked Birdie. 'I might, I do not know, but I am happy, happy, happy,' and she flicked with the feather broom and sang a trill. 'So happy,' sang Birdie. Emily had made her a flyaway apron with embroidery cotton strings that were pink like the carpet. 'My carpet,' sang Birdie. 'How I like pink! Trr-la! Trr-la! Trr-la-la!' How different was the sound of Birdie's 'la' from the walking doll's.

And Mr Plantaganet? Mr Plantaganet was different. He looked heavier, the porcelain of his face and hands seemed brighter, cleaner, the checks on his suit seemed more clearly marked, his red-ribbon tie more crisp. When he held his walking stick it looked as if he would swing it at any moment.

The house was a house to be proud of, well built, solid down to the last window sill and up to the wooden chimney. It was warm, gay, comfortable, and there was the lamp and its birthday cake candle for when it was dark. Emily and Charlotte often lit it, and when they had finished playing they shut the front and left the Plantaganets safe inside.

While Birdie dusted and Apple somersaulted on the stairs and Darner lay in his kennel, Mr Plantaganet sat in the sitting room reading the little papers Emily made for him and thinking what it would be like when the new chairs and curtains came. For the moment he had to sit on one of the bedroom chairs. He was quite happy, sitting in the sitting room, but he began to feel that, if he were a real master of the house he should, like Father, go to the office. 'I wish they would think of getting me an office,' said Mr Plantaganet. 'I should like to go to the office very much.'

They had kept a place for Tottie. There was a bed waiting for her in the same room as Apple, the room with the blue carpet. Mr Plantaganet slept with Birdie. Tottie's clothes were in the cupboard, her red knitted cloak hung in the hall with Birdie's straw hat with the feather. 'Of course we are all waiting for Tottie,' said Mr Plantaganet.

'Trr-la, trr-la, I wish Tottie were here,' sang Birdie. 'Then we could cook, little pretending flour pies and hundred-and-thousand sweets.' (Do you know hundreds-and-thousands? They make good dolls' house sweets.)

'If Tottie were here she wouldn't let me somersault downstairs, but I wish Tottie were here,' said Apple.

'It doesn't feel like our home without Tottie,' said Mr Plantaganet, then his face looked stiff and he dropped his walking stick. 'Birdie,' he said, 'suppose it isn't our home after all? Suppose we have made a mistake? They couldn't take it away from us, could they, Birdie?'

'I don't understand,' said Birdie, and she lowered her broom and the embroidery cotton strings of her apron sank and were still. 'What do you mean? I don't understand,' she said with a sound like a whimper.

'No. No. Don't think about it. I was only joking,' said Mr Plantaganet quickly.

'W-were you? It didn't sound like a joke.'

'Don't think about it. You go on with your dusting, my dear.'

'M-may I? Are you sure?'

'Of course, Birdie dear. Of course. Forget about it.'

Mr Plantaganet soon forgot about it himself. He had discovered that, when the birthday cake candle in the lamp was lit, the roses in the vase threw a tiny real shadow of themselves on the table.

# Chapter 12

The Exhibition was almost over. Many people had visited it; it was a great success.

Most of the people had taken notice of Tottie. 'What a love of a doll,' they had said. 'But that is what they say about Apple,' said Tottie. 'Oh, Apple. I long to see you again.'

Emily and Charlotte had been several times to visit her. 'Dear possession,' thought Tottie, 'a great treasure.' That was what Mrs Innisfree and the

Queen had said. Tottie could look them in the face now, happily. 'She doesn't look hurt any more,' said Emily.

'And we never found out why she did,' said Charlotte. 'That is the worst of dolls. They are such secret people.'

They showed Tottie a cutting from a newspaper. It gave an account of the Exhibition: '. . . *and the smallest doll is a hundred-year-old farthing doll, lent by Emily and Charlotte Dane.'* If anyone had listened, they might have heard a tiny gritting sound. It was Marchpane grinding her china teeth.

Emily and Charlotte had looked at Marchpane and admired her very much, especially Emily; they knew she had belonged to Great-Great-Aunt Laura, but they did not know she had lived with Tottie in the dolls' house.

Tottie was longing to go home, but the other dolls were, for the most part, sorry the Exhibition was over. They would be packed away again or sent back to their museums.

'What is a museum like?' asked Tottie.

'It is cold dere,' said the walking doll suddenly. She sounded quite unlike herself.

'Nonsense. It is grand and fine,' said March-pane. 'It is filled with precious and valuable things kept in glass cases.'

'I shouldn't enjoy that,' said Tottie, looking at Queen Victoria's dolls. 'How can you be played with if you are in a glass case?'

'One wouldn't want to be played with,' said Marchpane. 'When I was at the cleaners, people said I ought to be in a museum.'

'It is cold dere,' said the walking doll again.

'It is grand and fine,' said Marchpane.

'*C'est vrai mais –*' said the walking doll, '*Mais –*' Her voice sounded as if her works had quite run down.

'I don't want to go back in my box,' said the wax doll. 'It is too dark and quiet. I wish . . . ' She was thinking of the caretaker's child who still crept out to look at her in the evenings when the people had gone. 'I wish . . . '

The last day came. Tottie, with every minute, grew more happy and excited.

'You are lucky,' sighed the wax doll.

'Tell us about dis 'ouse you are in,' said the walking doll.

'Yes, tell us. Then I can think about it when I lie

with my eyes shut in my box. I can think and pretend. Tell, Tottie. Tell us.'

All the dolls took up the cry. 'Tell us, Tottie. Tell.'

Tottie had always thought it better not to talk about the house in front of Marchpane, but now she was so excited and happy herself and so sorry for the other dolls that she forgot to take care. She began to tell about the dolls' house.

She told them about its cream walls and the ivy and Darner's kennel. She told about the red hall and the sitting room with the holly-green carpet and the struggle to get the chairs (though she did not tell that she had thought that she herself had been sold to get them). She told about the rooms upstairs and the pink and blue carpets and the bath with the taps, and she told about Birdie and Mr Plantaganet and Darner and Apple. She told them from the beginning to the end, from the bottom to the top. When she had done, there was a long soft silence, and then a-aahs and sighs from the dolls.

'If only . . . '

'I wish . . . '

'It might have been . . . '

'I wish . . . '

'If only . . . '

'If only . . . '

'Oh, lucky, lucky Tottie!'

'Oh, Tottie, you are lucky!'

'Don't you believe her,' cried Marchpane in a loud voice. 'That isn't her house. It's mine.'

All the dolls looked at Marchpane. Then they all looked at Tottie.

'It is in our nursery now,' said Tottie.

'You stole it while I was at the cleaners.'

'It was sent to us, as you were sent to the cleaners. It needed cleaning and taking care of,' said Tottie. 'We cleaned it and took care of it.'

'How dare you!' cried Marchpane. 'You think because the Queen noticed you, you can do anything. Wait and see. Wait and see,' cried Marchpane. 'I shall have that house back.'

'How can you?' asked Tottie. 'It's in our nursery.'

'Wait and see,' said Marchpane. 'Wait and see.'

The Exhibition was closed. The dolls had been taken away, the room was empty, and when the caretaker's child came in the evening there were only long blank tables where Tottie and Marchpane and Queen Victoria's dolls and the walking doll and the wax doll and the other dolls had been.

Did the caretaker's child think of the wax doll?

And the wax doll, in her lonely box, think of the caretaker's child and of the finger that had touched her satin dress? Did the dolls think of Tottie's welcome home by Emily, Charlotte, Birdie, Mr Plantaganet, Apple, and Darner?

I think they did.

# Chapter 13

It was winter when Tottie came back to the dolls' house. If you would like to know how winter looks to a doll imagine yourself as looking into a crystal ball, a ball of glass, in which a Christmas-frost snowstorm is being shaken down on little splinter trees and cardboard houses. Children were given those snowstorm balls when Great-Great-Aunt Laura and Emily and Charlotte's great-grandmother were young. Winter looks like that to dolls because they are not often taken out in the winter, and they see the snow and snowflakes through the windowpanes of glass.

Tottie came back and it was winter, but so far there was no snow.

Emily and Charlotte took her with them when they went to Mrs Innisfree's house to fetch the couch and chairs.

'Tottie ought to go, because it was Tottie who really got the chairs for us,' said Emily.

'Are the couch and chairs really coming, Tottie?' asked Mr Plantaganet. 'We have been wishing and wishing. I have never really stopped wishing,' said Mr Plantaganet. 'But it was you who got them for us, Tottie,' he said.

'Dear Tottie, but I should have been quite content with cotton reels,' said Birdie.

'Oh, Birdie dear!' said Mr Plantaganet impatiently. Sometimes he found it hard to be patient with Birdie.

Apple was not there. He had a plan, unknown to Tottie, that he might climb up to the dolls' house chimney. He thought he might climb up the ivy, it looked so real, but of course it was painted too flat and the paint was far too slippery.

Emily made Tottie a cotton-wool cap and a

cotton-wool muff to go out in, as it was beginning to be bitterly cold. 'But we are cosy in the dolls' house,' said Mr Plantaganet. The whiteness of the cotton wool looked pretty with Tottie's glossy black hair and painted cheeks; she shone with happiness. Birdie did not want a cap or a muff. She wanted a feather boa.

'What's a boa?' asked Apple, forgetting the ivy.

'It's a long scarf, but made out of feathers, and it is round all the way down,' explained Tottie.

'Like a caterpillar?' asked Apple, who had seen a caterpillar in the park.

'Yes, a caterpillar would make a very good boa for Birdie,' said Tottie.

'If it were made out of feathers,' said Birdie. 'But it's not.'

Tottie was carried along to Mrs Innisfree's on the palm of Charlotte's hand. Charlotte had on a red woollen glove, Tottie had on her red woollen cloak, her cap and muff. They went well together.

It was a clear, pale, cold sunny day; the bare branches of the trees in the Park stood out against a clear pale sky. The cold touched Tottie's cheeks and the sunlight made them glisten.

Emily and Charlotte were talking of Christmas, and Tottie was suddenly reminded of a little sunshade, a parasol, not made, like the walking doll's parasol, from satin, but of paper from a cracker. 'I saw one long ago,' said Tottie. 'It was gay as a little paper wheel. How Birdie would love that,' thought Tottie. 'How I should like to give her one for Christmas. She would like it better than the feather boa, but you don't see them nowadays. I wish . . . ' said Tottie, sitting on Charlotte's hand; 'and for Apple a marble. A marble would make him a good ball, and for Darner a tiddlywinks plate, a nice big purple one. And for Mr Plantaganet? I wish they would think of getting him a toy post office,' thought Tottie. 'Then he could go to business; if he went to business every day he would be very happy. I wish and wish they would get him a toy post office.'

When they arrived in Mrs Innisfree's house, Tottie forgot even about Christmas and Christmas presents. There, on the table in Mrs Innisfree's drawing room, were the couch and chairs.

Emily did not recognize them.

Charlotte did not recognize them.

Tottie did not recognize them.

Their wood, having been carefully sand-papered, had been polished by Mrs Innisfree's French polisher until it shone with a real furniture dark wood shine of its own. Then the *petit-point* seats and arms and backs had been fastened over new cushions. Mrs Innisfree had worked the cream background and the tiny roses and leaves; she had even worked their shadings, though the flowers were scarcely bigger than knots or dots.

'Oh!' cried Emily.

'Oh!' cried Charlotte.

'Oh!' cried Tottie. 'Oh! It was worth going to the Exhibition.'

'Even the Queen's dolls' house,' said Emily, 'hasn't a better set than that.'

'Yes, that is perfectly right,' said Tottie. She felt now she knew something about queens.

Mrs Innisfree put down on the table two pairs of fine white lace curtains, each curtain six inches long. 'I saw the piece of lace,' she said. 'It was the right width and just the right length, and there is a piece, three inches, over, so I made an apron for Tottie. Do you see, Emily, the lace is worked with ferns? Your great-grandmother's drawing room might easily have had lace curtains worked with ferns. They were very fashionable then.'

'We shall keep them always, we shall never change them,' said Emily solemnly. 'Nor will our children's children.'

'Do you suppose Tottie will see them?' asked Charlotte. 'I mean our children's children, not the chairs.'

'She may,' said Emily.

'That makes me think,' said Charlotte, and she added, 'I seem to have been thinking a great deal of thinking lately.

It was a solemn morning. Mrs Innisfree and Emily did an account and it seemed that the cost of the lace curtains, of Mrs Innisfree's French polisher and upholsterer, and of the silks and canvas for the chairs, came to eight and tenpence, which was just the money they had had in their money boxes, though Charlotte now had the sixpence for her tooth and Emily had saved another half-crown.

'I believe you are saying eight and tenpence,' said Emily, looking hard at Mrs Innisfree, 'because you knew it was eight and tenpence that we had,' said Emily.

'And if I am?' said Mrs Innisfree. 'If I enjoy it?'

'And we can't pay you for the time,' said Charlotte, 'nor for the thinking. I wonder what makes thinking,' said Charlotte. 'It is funny how one thing begins another.'

'And how it all leads on,' said Emily.

'Yes, it joins,' said Charlotte, wrinkling her forehead. 'I have been thinking of thinking. And there is no knowing where it leads to, or when it will end, or where.'

# Chapter 14

On Christmas morning the Plantaganets woke to hear real carol singers in the street outside.

'*Peace and goodwill among men,*' sang the carol singers.

'And among dolls,' said Mr Plantaganet. 'I hope among dolls.'

'*Peace and goodwill.*' The voices brought Christmas into the dolls' house. 'Can such a large thing as Christmas be in a dolls' house?' asked Mr

Plantaganet. 'It is so large. See, it has spread over the whole world, and for so many years, nearly two thousand years,' said Mr Plantaganet, the dark brown of his eyes looking large too. 'How large it is,' said Mr Plantaganet.

'It is beautifully small too,' said Tottie. 'Perfectly small.'

You might think that, to a doll, many things would seem too large, but no. A doll is not as small as a beetle, for instance, and a beetle's world is just right for a beetle. When, too, you have lived as long as Tottie, you will learn that small things are not as small as they seem, nor large things as large; nothing is small and nothing is large when you have become accustomed to the world. Now the carols brought the spirit of Christmas into the dolls' house.

'I like "Peace and Goodwill",' said Tottie.

'I like "The Holly and the Ivy",' said Mr Plantaganet. 'They are like the colours in this house. I like "Prince of Peace"; that suits it too. I know about peace now,' said Mr Plantaganet. 'In the days of the toy cupboard –' he began and his eyes looked darker and he did not go on. 'Yes, I like "The Prince of Peace", but the one that I like best of all is "God

Bless the Master of This House", because I am the Master,' said Mr Plantaganet.

Birdie liked the rocking carol, only she mixed it with 'Rock-a-Bye Baby', but after all it was nearly the same thing.

*'Peace and goodwill,'* sang the carol singers.

The dolls' house, that Christmas, looked very pleasant. Emily and Charlotte had decorated it; they made wreaths of moss on curtain rings, that looked like holly wreaths, and they had strung holly berries for garlands. Emily had even made a paper chain with very small links. Birdie liked the paper chain best of anything. The new chairs and couch looked handsome in the drawing room, and there was a Christmas tree, six inches high, standing in a wooden pot. It was the kind of Christmas tree you have on Christmas cakes; it was just right for the Plantaganets.

'Would you like to give one of the Plantaganets this for Christmas?' asked the children's mother, coming into the room. 'I must have had it at a party long ago.' She showed them a parasol made of white paper printed with a pattern of purple and scarlet feathers. It could be put up and down, and had once fitted into a cracker.

'Oh! For Birdie,' cried Emily at once.

'How odd,' thought Tottie. 'How lovely and how odd.'

'And for Apple, a marble. Wouldn't a marble make a ball for Apple?'

'More and more odd,' thought Tottie, 'and still more lovely.'

'Darner might have a new plate,' said Charlotte, looking in the toy cupboard. 'This big tiddlywinks would do. The rest are all lost. It's a purple one. That would suit him nicely.'

'More and more odd,' thought Tottie again, 'and more and more lovely.'

For Mr Plantaganet they hung a buttonhole on the tree. It was made of woollen flowers. 'I don't much like that,' thought Tottie.

Mr Plantaganet did not much like it either. 'Is my Christmas spoilt?' he whispered to Tottie.

'No. *No*,' said Tottie. 'But I wish I could make it better.'

'I wish that too,' said Mr Plantaganet. He suspected it was spoilt.

At that moment the postman's knock sounded from the front door. Emily and Charlotte ran to open it. He had brought two parcels, a light thin one, the shape of a flat cardboard box, and a small one, the shape of a child's shoe-box. It was very heavy.

Emily opened the flat light one first.

'What is it?' asked Charlotte. 'What is it? Oh!' she cried as Emily set up a cardboard counter painted with netting. 'Oh! It's a post office. A toy post office.'

'Oh!' cried Tottie, and she caught Mr Plantaganet's eye.

'Look at the stamps,' said Emily, 'and the stamper.'

'Let me look at the stamps,' cried Mr Plantaganet.

'Let me look at the stamper,' cried Apple.

The toy post office was complete. It even had two letter boxes labelled PACKETS AND NEWS-PAPERS and LETTERS. It had stamps and certificates and postal orders and telegraph forms and letter paper and postcards and stamped envelopes. It had a red tin telephone and a purple inkpad for the stamper.

'But what shall we do with it exactly?' asked Charlotte.

'We can tell you,' wished Tottie and Mr

Plantaganet together, and Emily, as if she had felt them wishing, looked at them. Then she looked only at Mr Plantaganet. 'I know,' said Emily slowly. 'I know, Charlotte. It shall be Mr Plantaganet's office. He shall go there to business every day.'

'As a postman?' asked Charlotte.

'As a postmaster,' said Emily.

'A postmaster!' said Mr Plantaganet, and his waistcoat seemed to swell and grow bigger. 'Did you hear, Tottie? I am a post*master*. Did you hear, Birdie dear? Now I have nothing left to wish for. Did you hear, Apple? Oh, how happy I am. Did you hear –' He was about to say, 'Did you hear, Darner?' when he remembered that Darner was a dog and could not be expected to recognize the difference between Mr Plantaganet, Postmaster, and plain Mr Plantaganet. He stopped. His attention was caught by Darner.

Darner was looking at the other parcel. All his wool stood on end. 'Prrickckckck,' said Darner at the parcel. 'Prrick. Prrick. Prrick! Prrick! Prrrrrrickckckck!'

# Chapter 15

At the moment Darner barked at the parcel the Plantaganet family were all in the post office that Emily had set up on the table. Apple was playing with the scales, Birdie was tinkling the telephone; it had a bell and Birdie liked the sound of it. She wondered if a musical box sounded like that. Tottie had told her about musical boxes and she often longed to hear one. Tottie was looking at the postcards. Mr Plantaganet was trying not to wish that they would all go away and leave him alone with it.

As Darner barked, Tottie remembered the other parcel, and for no reason that she could put a name to, she found herself wishing and wishing and wishing that Emily would put them all back in the house. She must have wished very purposively, as Emily raised her head and said, 'I think they must all go back into the dolls' house now.'

'In the house, and behind the door. Shut the door,' wished Tottie.

'After all, Mr Plantaganet wouldn't go to the office on Christmas Day,' said Emily.

'Wouldn't he?' asked Mr Plantaganet.

'Wouldn't a postmaster? The postman does,' said Charlotte.

'A postman doesn't go the office,' said Emily, 'he goes on his rounds. You can't send parcels on Christmas Day, you only get them.'

'I wish you didn't,' said Tottie. She felt worried, a little frightened and a little angry; she felt as if her wood had gone stiff.

Charlotte put the Plantaganets tidily back in the house: Apple on the stairs, ready to somersault; Birdie in her bedroom, with the pink carpet, taking off her hat with the feather; Mr Plantaganet on one of the new chairs in the sitting room; and Tottie in the kitchen. 'Now you are all in your happy little house,' said Charlotte. She did not close the front.

'Our happy little house,' sang Apple as he began his somersaults. He reached the bottom and to his great joy Charlotte looked up and said, 'Oh, he has fallen downstairs, poor little Apple,' and put him up again.

'Our happy little house,' sang Birdie, twirling her feather.

'Our happy little house,' hummed Mr Plantaganet, 'and office,' he hummed as he read his paper. He went on humming: sometimes 'The Holly and the Ivy', sometimes 'Peace and Goodwill among Men'.

Charlotte had given Tottie the pudding basin tied in a scrap of white muslin and said she was turning out the Christmas pudding, but Tottie felt too nervous to think about puddings. She could hear Darner in his kennel still saying 'Prrick,' and Darner never said 'Prrickck' except for danger.

Through the open front of the dolls' house Tottie watched Emily undo that parcel.

Emily undid the string and then carefully she unwrapped the paper. It was a small shoe-box.

Tottie shivered all through her wood. 'Shoe-boxes are unlucky for this family,' she said. 'The last shoe-box made Mr Plantaganet awfully unhappy.'

The shoe-box was padded with cotton wool and paper. Emily and Charlotte lifted it out, piece by piece, and then Emily gave a cry of admiration and pleasure. 'Look, Charlotte. Look. It's a doll. That doll. That lovely doll.' And she lifted Marchpane from the box.

There was a sudden light clatter in the dolls' house kitchen, but nobody heard.

'Oh! I loved her at the Exhibition,' cried Emily. 'You remember her, Charlotte. She has been sent to us because she was Great-Great-Aunt Laura's doll. Look, the letter says she would have come before only she was sent to the cleaners and the Exhibition. She goes with the dolls' house, you see.'

'Does she?' asked Charlotte doubtfully. She looked at Marchpane and then at the Plantaganets so happily settled in the dolls' house. Emily had no eyes for anyone but Marchpane. 'Look at her clothes,' said Emily.

'My clothes,' said Marchpane in a complacent voice.

'They take off and on. Look at the tiny buttons and the lace edgings.'

'The lace edgings,' said Marchpane still more complacently.

'And her hair! We can really brush it and comb it.'

'It's real hair,' said Marchpane.

'And her eyes. Look. They open and shut. None of the others' can open and shut.'

'Mine open and shut. They are the best blue glass,' said Marchpane.

'She doesn't smell very nice,' said Charlotte.

'Oh, Charlotte. I loved her at the Exhibition,' said Emily, 'and now she is ours.'

'I don't remember her very well at the Exhibition,' said Charlotte slowly. 'She wasn't ours then and we went there to see Tottie.'

'Yes, but we looked at her.'

'I didn't. I looked at Tottie.'

'Don't be such a little silly, Charlotte,' said Emily. 'What is the matter with you?'

'I don't know,' said Charlotte. 'I have a funny feeling.'

'Well, you are very silly. She is perfectly beautiful. She must be our best doll.'

'But –' began Charlotte, and then she said in a low voice, 'Do you think we ought to have a best doll, Emily? Do you think it is kind to the others? They were here first.'

'No, they were not,' said Emily. 'Marchpane was Great-Great-Aunt Laura's doll.'

'Well, Tottie was our great-grandmother's doll,' said Charlotte, and then she gave a cry. 'Oh, Emily, look! Tottie has dropped the Christmas pudding bowl down on the floor and it has rolled right under the kitchen table.'

## Chapter 16

They brought Marchpane into the dolls' house.

Tottie stood by the kitchen table, stiff and hard. 'It was nearly I, and not the pudding, that fell,' thought Tottie. 'I fell once, for joy, but I shall not fall for fear of Marchpane. Trees, good trees, don't fall down in storms,' said Tottie.

Charlotte picked up the pudding basin and, as it was lunch time, she untied the muslin and turned out a morsel of real plum pudding onto a plate. 'I wish I could give you a sprig of holly small enough to stick in it,' said Charlotte kindly.

Emily brought Marchpane into the kitchen first. 'You should remember each other,' she said to Tottie.

'We remember each other,' said Marchpane and Tottie. Tottie had never looked more wooden. Marchpane's eyeballs gave a sudden click.

'You jerked her,' said Emily to Charlotte.

'No I didn't,' said Charlotte.

'Of course, they first knew each other years and years ago,' said Emily. 'They must know secrets about each other that we don't know.'

'We do,' said Tottie. Marchpane said nothing at all.

Presently Emily took her into the sitting room and sat her on the couch by Mr Plantaganet, and then she shut the front of the dolls' house and went away to lunch.

When Mr Plantaganet saw Marchpane sitting opposite him with her golden hair and blue eyes and white clothes, he was quite dazzled. He dropped his newspaper and stared with both his dark glass eyes.

'Don't do that,' said Marchpane sharply.

'Don't do what?'

'Stare and stare and stare,' said Marchpane. 'It's very rude.'

'I am sorry,' said Mr Plantaganet politely, 'but I can't help staring.'

'I suppose they are fixed,' said Marchpane, looking at him.

'Fixed?'

'They don't open and shut?'

'Open and shut?'

'Your eyes,' said Marchpane. 'Take them off me at once.'

'Excuse me,' said Mr Plantaganet still more politely, 'my eyes are not on you. They are in me.'

'Faugh!' said Marchpane. 'You should be in the hall, not sitting in a chair. If you sit at all, it should be in the kitchen.'

'Excuse me,' said Mr Plantaganet again as he grew more and more bewildered. 'Why should I be in the hall and kitchen? Why shouldn't I sit? I'm jointed.'

'Are you not the butler?' asked Marchpane. 'There used to be a butler, I'm sure.'

'The figure of a butler,' Mr Plantaganet corrected her. 'He is gone to dust. I don't know what a butler is,' said Mr Plantaganet, 'but I know I am not one.

I am a postmaster, and, besides, I am the master of this house. Do you know that carol?' he asked, '*"God bless the Master of this House, God bless the Mistress too"*? Well, I am the master and Birdie is the mistress.'

'That she certainly is not,' said Marchpane.

'Oh yes, she is,' said Mr Plantaganet positively.

'She isn't. I am,' said Marchpane.

'You?' asked Mr Plantaganet. 'Oh no! How could you be? I have never seen you before and I have seen Birdie. Do you know who I thought you were? I thought you might be the fairy off the Christmas tree. Birdie is always talking about her. Are you the fairy off a Christmas tree?'

'A fairy?' said Marchpane scornfully. 'I am real. Far more real than Birdie.'

'Does Birdie know that?' asked Mr Plantaganet anxiously.

There was a sudden bump, bump, bump, on the other side of the wall.

What is that?' asked Marchpane.

'That is Apple.'

'Apple?'

'The little boy doll. Our little boy. He belongs to us.'

'Does he?' asked Marchpane thoughtfully.

There was a light sound of rustling from upstairs.

'What is that?' asked Marchpane.

'That is Birdie.'

'It is too light,' objected Marchpane, 'to be an anyone.'

'Birdie is light,' answered Mr Plantaganet.

'I am heavy,' said Marchpane.

Mr Plantaganet did not answer. The rustling sound came again.

'What is she doing?' asked Marchpane.

'I expect she is dusting the paper chains with her feather broom,' said Mr Plantaganet.

'Paper chains? With a feather broom? What a very odd thing to do! What did you say her name was?'

'Birdie.'

'It does sound like a bird rustling,' said Marchpane.

Mr Plantaganet thought of that and it seemed to him that Marchpane was right and Birdie was, truthfully, very like a bird, a small light bird with thin legs and bright eyes. 'One that goes for short flights,' thought Mr Plantaganet. 'One that collects bits of things to make its nest.' Yes, Birdie in her bedroom, busy with her private affairs, twig after twig, was very like a bird building its nest.

'It's an aggravating noise,' said Marchpane.

'I like to hear her,' answered Mr Plantaganet, and his voice sounded as if he were smiling.

'I wish you would stop her.'

'Oh no,' said Mr Plantaganet. 'I shouldn't like to disturb her.'

'I shall disturb her!' said Marchpane.

'But – you wouldn't. You couldn't,' cried Mr Plantaganet in alarm.

'Why not?' asked Marchpane.

'It – it is cruel to disturb a bird in its nest,' said Mr Plantaganet. That was not what he had meant to say but it seemed to say that he wanted even better than the words he had meant to use.

'Faugh!' said Marchpane and the blue glass balls of her eyes seemed to glare. Mr Plantaganet felt quite frightened. 'Oh!' yawned Marchpane. 'I do wish Emily and Charlotte, or whatever their names are, would come and put me in my own room.'

At that, a thought came into Mr Plantaganet's mind. A horrible thought. To make quite sure he went, in his mind, through the whole dolls' house, through the kitchen and hall, sitting room, and the upstairs pink room and blue room. Then he looked at Marchpane. 'Excuse me,' said Mr

Plantaganet timidly, 'but – er – which is your room?'

'The one with the pink carpet of course,' said Marchpane.

'But that is Birdie's. She chose it. That is Birdie's nest.' He meant to say 'room' but he was so upset that he was confused and again 'nest' seemed to suit Birdie even better than 'room.' That is Birdie's nest–bedroom.'

'If you really want to know,' said Marchpane in her flat, heavy voice, 'the whole house is mine.'

'Wh-a-t?' cried poor Mr Plantaganet. He could not believe his little porcelain ears. 'But it's our house. Ours. That we dreamed of – that we wanted – that we wished for,' said Mr Plantaganet.

'I can't help what you did for it,' said Marchpane, yawning. 'It is mine. Mine, and really,' said Marchpane, yawning again, 'I can't live in it with all these people, bumping and rustling and having silly ideas that it is theirs. I must tell Emily and Charlotte,' said Marchpane, and she yawned still once again.

'Oh, don't say that. Don't say that,' cried poor little Mr Plantaganet.

'But I do say it,' said Marchpane.

'But – you don't understand. This is our house. It is full of us. It was for us. We were on the hearthrug when the letter came. We saw Emily and Charlotte clean it and make it new again and we helped them by wishing. We wished so hard – you don't know. We waited for the curtains and the blankets on the beds and the couch and chairs. You don't know. Now I shall go every day to the office and come back again . . . And this Christmas was so beautiful. You don't know,' panted Mr Plantaganet, 'oh, truly, truly you don't know.'

'What you don't know, and had better know,' said Marchpane, 'is that I was here, here in this dolls' house, long, long years ago. Long, long before any of you.'

'Not before Tottie you weren't' said Mr Plantaganet, and as he said it his eyes grew steady and his voice grew suddenly firm. 'Tottie has been here as long as you have. Why, she remembers your coming. She has been here longer.'

'Tottie! A farthing doll!'

'A farthing, or a penny, or sixpence, or a pound, she has been here longer. Tottie is Tottie. She always is and she always had been. Tottie! Tottie! Tottie!' called Mr Plantaganet.

At that moment Charlotte opened the front of the dolls' house and picked up Tottie.

'I don't see,' said Charlotte, 'why you should be left all alone in the kitchen while she sits on one of your chairs. You shall come into the sitting room, Tottie,' and she sat Tottie down on the couch next to Marchpane. 'There,' said Charlotte to Marchpane, and shut the dolls' house front again.

'Did you hear what she said?' whispered Mr Plantaganet to Tottie as soon as Charlotte had gone. In his agitation he had lost his manners, but Tottie had not lost hers.

'How strange it must seem to you to be back,' she said to Marchpane. ('Yes, I heard,' she said quietly to Mr Plantaganet.)

'Did you hear what she said about Birdie, and our house, our dear, dear house? Oh, Tottie! Oh, Tottie! I feel as if we were in danger,' said Mr Plantaganet.

'We are in danger,' thought Tottie, but she did not say it aloud because she knew Marchpane must not know they were in the least frightened. Instead she thought of all the bravest things that were made of wood: the bowsprits and figureheads of ships, for instance, that have to drive into the sea and meet the waves: or their masts; of the stocks of rifles and of guns; of flagstaffs that fly flags high up in the air, and of her tree. 'I am made of the same stuff as they,' thought Tottie. 'Wood. Good strong wood. After all, nothing very strong is made of kid.' She smiled at Mr Plantaganet and he felt as though she had reached out and patted his hand and said 'Courage.' She smiled at Marchpane and said again, 'How strange for you to be back.'

'Not nearly as strange as for you,' said Marchpane.

'Why?' asked Tottie.

'One hardly expected you to last for so long.'

'Why?' asked Tottie.

'Cheap material, shoddy stuff.'

'Wood is neither cheap nor shoddy,' said Tottie, and again she thought of the bowsprits, the gun stocks, flagstaffs, trees, and she smiled.

'Don't you mind what she says?' asked Mr Plantaganet.

'No, I don't mind because it isn't true,' said Tottie. 'I can remember the day they brought you here,' she said, turning to Marchpane. 'When Laura brought you here. Those two little girls!' she said.

'Sometimes I think Emily and Charlotte are they all over again.'

'Funny how people don't last,' said Marchpane, yawning. 'But I am tired. Don't talk to me about them. I am not interested in little girls.'

'Not – interested – in – little – girls!' said Mr Plantaganet, shocked.

'No. Not in Laura, nor her sister, nor Emily, nor Charlotte, nor any of them,' said Marchpane distinctly.

'But they are alive! It is only they who make us live.'

'Faugh!' said Marchpane rudely.

'Marchpane doesn't like to be played with,' said Tottie quietly.

'Not like to be played with? Then what is she for? Why was she made? I should sooner be broken,' said Mr Plantaganet, 'or thrown in the toy cupboard, then never be played with at all.'

'Well, I shouldn't,' said Marchpane.

'You are not a doll,' cried Mr Plantaganet; he had forgotten to be frightened. 'You are a *thing*.' And then he remembered and cried, 'Oh, what are we going to do, Tottie?'

'We must wish,' said Tottie openly; she was no

longer trying to be polite to Marchpane. 'We must wish and we must never stop wishing for a moment.'

'I can wish too,' said Marchpane. 'I am heavier than you!'

'To be heavy doesn't mean to be strong,' said Tottie.

'I am very strong.'

'Nothing, nothing,' said Tottie, 'nothing can be stronger than good plain wood.'

# Chapter 17

'Charlotte,' said Emily, 'we must take Birdie and Mr Plantaganet out of the pink bedroom. We need it for Marchpane.

'But,' began Charlotte, 'you gave it to them.'

'Well, where is she to go? Would you put her in the attic?'

'N-no, but where are *they* to go?'

'Marchpane will need that big bed all to herself,' said Emily. 'They must go in with Tottie and Apple.'

'There isn't room.'

'Then they must go in the attic.'

'There isn't even a bed, Emily.'

'There is a cotton-reel box,' said Emily. 'They must sleep in that. We can make it quite pretty for them.'

So, instead of their room and their brass, painted bed Birdie and Mr Plantaganet were put to sleep in the attic in a cardboard box with *J. Coats Ltd., Manchester*, on its side. Emily did not take much interest in it, but Charlotte made a mattress of cotton wool and tried to nick round the edges of blankets, but her hands were small and clumsy. 'Oh dear! It doesn't look nice,' said Charlotte.

There was not even time to warn Birdie. Emily turned all her clothes and her apron out of the cupboard and cut down the paper chains. 'Marchpane doesn't go with paper chains,' said Emily, and she swept them all into the attic before anyone could say a word of warning to Birdie.

'What will she do? What will she say? My poor Birdie,' cried Mr Plantaganet. 'She will never understand.' But, oddly enough, Birdie understood only too well.

'Of course,' said Birdie, 'she couldn't sleep in a cotton-reel box, could she? Her eyes open and shut and her hair is yellow like mine, only it's real –'

'Yes,' said Mr Plantaganet. 'When I first saw her I thought she was a Christmas tree fairy.'

'Did you?' asked Birdie and, for the first time, her voice sounded wistful. 'I suppose – I am never – anything like a Christmas fairy?' There was silence, and then Birdie said in her own brisk light voice, 'After all, I came from a cracker box, why shouldn't I sleep in a cotton-reel box?' The words 'cracker box' and 'cotton-reel box' began to knock one another gently in her head. 'I came from a cotton-reel box. Why shouldn't I sleep in a cracker box? Cotton box, cracker box, cracker-reel box?'

'You are getting muddled,' said Mr Plantaganet, 'and remember, Birdie, don't go into her room.'

Birdie could not remember. She was always being found in Marchpane's room, still thinking it was hers.

'Don't you like my pink carpet?' she would ask Marchpane.

'My pink carpet,' said Marchpane.

'No mine,' said Birdie. 'Certainly. Emily and Charlotte gave it to me.'

'It wasn't theirs to give.'

'Isn't everything theirs?' asked Birdie in astonishment.

'Faugh! Get out of my room.'

'My room,' cried poor Birdie.

'My room, my carpet, my bed. Get back to your cotton-reel box.'

'She is cruel,' said Mr Plantaganet, trembling. 'She is cruel. I hate her.'

'Don't waste time hating,' said Tottie. 'You must wish. I wish. We must wish.' But the wishing showed no sign of changing anything, or perhaps Marchpane was wishing harder. Emily was now doing everything for Marchpane, nothing for the Plantaganets, though Charlotte tried to prevent this.

'Charlotte is on our side,' said Tottie.

'Yes, but Emily isn't, and Emily is the one who does things, far more than Charlotte.'

'Emily has the ideas, she thinks of things and does them while Charlotte is far behind. If you go ahead like that, sometimes you must go wrong. Think if you were ahead, walking, on a road by yourself, and there were not any signposts,' said Tottie. 'Sometimes you must make a mistake. It is easy for the one to come behind and say, "This was wrong, that was wrong." They only know it was wrong because Emily went there first. They know the right way. They don't have to choose. Emily often chooses wrong things,' said Tottie, 'but I know Emily. She has plenty of sense. We must be patient, and go on wishing. One day Emily will find out she is wrong.'

'She will find out that Marchpane isn't the beautiful doll she seems? That she is a thing?' asked Mr Plantaganet.

'Yes, she will.'

'You are – certain, Tottie?'

'Certain,' said Tottie in her most wooden voice.

# Chapter 18

Perhaps Marchpane was very powerful or Emily had less sense than Tottie thought; at all events, she showed no sign of changing and things grew worse and worse for the Plantaganets.

'I know,' said Emily one day. 'Let us pretend they are the servants. They can sleep in the attic and stay in the kitchen. Let them be Marchpane's servants.'

'Oh no! Emily, oh no!' said Charlotte, shocked. 'How can they be? They are themselves.

Marchpane is more like their aunt or their step-sister.'

'She isn't like a sister,' said Emily, and that was certainly true. 'She is a lady. A great lady. I don't want them in the sitting room with her.'

'Why shouldn't they be in the sitting room?'

'They are so ordinary. So like ordinary people.'

'Then I like ordinary people.'

'Yes, but they don't go with Marchpane.' Emily had her way, and the Plantaganets were told to keep in the kitchen.

Mr Plantaganet couldn't understand it. 'The master of the house to stay in the kitchen, not to go into the sitting room, not to go where he likes in his own house? Father goes where he likes. I am the father, the master of the house, Tottie?'

'Of course you are,' said Tottie firmly.

'I am not – what she called me, Tottie? I am not the butler, am I?'

'You shan't be the butler,' said Tottie, but Emily put in her hand and took up Mr Plantaganet. 'You are the butler,' said Emily. 'Go and open the door.'

'I am a postmaster, the master of the house, post-master, house master,' cried poor Mr Plantaganet, struggling.

'A pretty postmaster!' said Marchpane. 'Emily hasn't opened your post office for days.'

'Shouldn't we put up the post office for Mr Plantaganet?' suggested Charlotte.

'He can't have it now,' said Emily. 'He is being the butler. And Birdie can be cook.'

'But – would Birdie make a very good cook?' asked Charlotte miserably. 'You know how muddled she gets. Suppose she were muddled between sugar and salt.'

'Or coffee and curry power, or beans and sultanas.' Emily laughed, but the Plantaganets did not laugh. 'Very well, she can be the maid and Tottie can be the cook.'

'Tottie – can – be – the – cook?' said Charlotte, reeling.

'Yes, we can make her a dear little cap and apron.'

'But Tottie – Tottie, Emily!'

'I don't care,' said Emily in a hard voice. 'I want a cook for Marchpane and Tottie must be cook. I don't see anything in it,' said Emily loudly. 'We often make her cook.' Charlotte was silent. 'Don't we?' said Emily more loudly. 'She likes cooking.'

Charlotte was silent. 'I don't care,' said Emily again. 'She is the cook, so there!'

'You have to do as you think with dolls,' she said to Charlotte's silent face. 'You have to play with them.'

'Yes, poor dolls,' said Charlotte.

'I'm only playing with them,' said Emily defiantly.

'Yes, poor dolls,' said Charlotte.

# Chapter 19

Now the Plantaganets, of the dolls' house, were only allowed to use the attic and kitchen. Marchpane lay in their big bed, bathed in their bath, sat on their chairs, ate and drank out of their flowered china, looked out of their windows. She sat by the lamp and saw the shadow of the roses; she had Birdie's birdcage, and her feather broom. If Birdie's hat had fitted on her head, you can be sure Emily would have given it to her.

And Apple? Apple was still Apple in the house. He would not stay in the kitchen, not because, like Birdie, he could not remember, but because he did not want to stay in the kitchen.

'You are naughty, Apple,' said Tottie.

'I want to be naughty,' said Apple.

He was not afraid of Marchpane. He did not dislike her. He was not afraid of anybody, and he liked everybody as everybody liked him. 'Sing me a song,' he said to Marchpane, as he would have said to Birdie and Tottie.

'I don't know any songs,' said Marchpane, and Apple laughed in high delight because he thought Marchpane was teasing. 'Go on, sing it,' said Apple.

But Marchpane really did not know any songs. She had lived for all those years in nurseries and she did not know any songs. This was because her head was so filled up with thoughts of herself that there was no room for the smallest song to enter; but she was very clever. She knew that the Plantaganets did not like Apple to be with her and so she said, 'You sing to me.' This was clever because most people, however small, like to sing their own songs best, and Apple began to sing to Marchpane. Every day he sang her a song and she pretended to love it. Soon he had a habit of going in to Marchpane.

'Apple, don't do that,' said Tottie.

'Will,' said Apple.

'Don't,' said Tottie.

'Don't,' said Mr Plantaganet.

'Don't, don't, don't,' said Birdie.

'Do,' said Marchpane, 'do.'

Apple liked people who said 'do' better than people who said 'don't' and he continued to go in to Marchpane.

'She will get him into mischief,' said Tottie.

'I am very uneasy about him,' said Mr Plantaganet, but they were far too proud to go in after Apple and show Marchpane they cared. Birdie was not too proud. She went straight in and brought Apple back. That surprised them.

'There were no two thoughts about it,' said Birdie, and she looked surprised herself. 'Sometimes there are not,' she said. 'Sometimes there is only one thought and then I know what to do. Sometimes, but not very often.'

'And why don't you let him play with me?' asked Marchpane.

Birdie could not answer. As soon as Marchpane spoke to her, she became confused, and thought of heaviness and lightness, and yellow hair that was not real and was real, and eyes that were painted and eyes that opened and shut, and wedding clothes and cracker feathers and the fairy off the Christmas tree. She could not speak to Marchpane, but Tottie answered her.

'Because we do not choose,' said Tottie.

'*You* do not choose?'

'You let him do dangerous things,' said Birdie suddenly.

'Do I?' asked Marchpane and smiled. 'Yes, I do,' she said, 'if I want.'

'You had better not,' said Tottie. 'He is our little boy.'

'Is he? Fancy that!' said Marchpane. She glared at Tottie. 'Wait and see,' said Marchpane. 'Wait and see, you little splinter!'

Suddenly, just after that, Emily said to Charlotte, 'I know, Apple shall be her little boy.'

'Whose little boy?'

'Marchpane's.'

'Marchpane's?'

'Yes. Marchpane's.'

'But he isn't Marchpane's little boy. He is a Plantaganet. You can't change him now.'

'Why can't I?'

'You can't. I won't have it,' said Charlotte.

'Charlotte, who is the Eldest?'

'You can't be the Eldest all the time,' cried poor Charlotte.

In the dolls' house there was silence. Marchpane, Birdie, Mr Plantaganet, Tottie, and Darner had all heard. Apple was not listening; he had made a white gumboot out of the little bedroom jug and was trying it on his foot over his red shoe and now he could not get it off.

Darner was the first to break the silence. 'Prrick!' said Darner. 'Prrick! Prrick! Prrick!'

'Did you hear?' asked Mr Plantaganet then, in a long, long whisper. 'Tottie, did you hear?'

'Did I hear? Or did you? Did I? Did you? Did I?' said Birdie, rattling terribly.

Tottie did not answer. She was wishing desperately, her wood as hard as if were full of knots and grains. 'Oh, Emily! Emily! Emily! Emily! I wish. I wish. I wish,' wished Tottie. 'Oh, Emily. Emily!'

But Marchpane only smiled her heavy china smile.

# *Chapter 20*

If it were impossible for Birdie to remember that her room was Marchpane's, how could she remember that Apple was now Marchpane's little boy? She forgot all the time and this, of course, gave Marchpane many opportunities to pounce on her, and Marchpane loved pouncing on Birdie. 'She is like a cat with a poor little bird,' said Mr Plantaganet indignantly. 'Oh, I hate to see her,' and he begged Birdie, 'Birdie, do try and remember.

Remember that your room is her room. Remember that Apple is her little boy.'

'You say that?' said Birdie.

'I have to say it,' said Mr Plantaganet sadly.

'I shall never say it,' said Birdie.

Tottie looked at her. 'Birdie, do you try and not remember?' she asked.

Birdie did not answer.

'But she is so cruel to you,' said Mr Plantaganet.

'Yes,' said Birdie, 'but I don't mind. I don't remember it.'

Tottie and Mr Plantaganet looked at her. 'How strange Birdie is,' they were both thinking. 'She looks as if she had grown lighter,' thought Mr Plantaganet. 'And how untidy she is. No wonder Marchpane teases her. She looks as if she had forgotten about her hair and her apron strings, and the feather on her hat and her parasol. She looks as if she might fly away. And how bright she looks,' thought Mr Plantaganet, 'like someone standing near a candle.'

'Like a doll in a lit shop window,' thought Tottie. 'Like a doll on a Christmas tree,' thought Mr Plantaganet.

'Birdie, do try and remember,' urged Tottie. 'Try and

remember not to go in after Apple. We must give him up for the present. Just for the present,' said Tottie firmly. 'We shall get him back,' said Tottie.

Mr Plantaganet was too sad to speak. Darner did not even growl, but turned over in his kennel with a sharp little flop; Birdie said nothing, nor did that bright look on her face alter at all.

It happened that Mrs Innisfree gave Emily and Charlotte a musical box. It was a small wooden one, painted with kittens and fans, and it was made in Switzerland. When it was wound up, it played music that was the smallest tinkle, delicate and thin. Emily had put it in the dolls' house sitting room for Marchpane and Apple to hear, and the sound of it filled the house. 'Tinkle, tinkle,' played the musical box. It drew Birdie form the kitchen.

'What is it? What is it?' asked Birdie. 'Oh, how beautiful! How beautiful it is!' It seemed to her more beautiful than anything she had ever heard or ever imagined. 'It is like the songs I meant my bird to sing, only I didn't know them then. How could I know? I am only a cracker doll, but I know now,' said Birdie. 'I know now.'

It drew her from the kitchen across the hall to the closed sitting-room door.

Birdie had tried to remember what Tottie and Mr Plantaganet had asked. For two whole days she had not followed Apple, not gone into her bedroom, not gone near Marchpane. Now, as she stood at the sitting-room door, the tinkling of the musical box delighted her so much that it tinkled in her head and she could no longer remember what anyone had said.

She had no idea of going in, nor of anything else but the music, when suddenly she heard a sound that upset the running of the tinkling and spoilt it.

'Oh, hush!' said Birdie. 'Don't, don't.'

She tried to listen to the music again, but again came that ugly sound.

'No!' said Birdie. 'Hush. Hush.'

But it came again. Again. Suddenly Birdie, as if she had woken up, knew clearly what it was. It was Darner barking. 'Prrick,' came the sound. 'Prrick! Prrick! Prrick!'

Clearly, in that instant, Birdie had one thought, and only one. 'That was Darner,' thought Birdie clearly, 'Darner barking. Some-thing is happening to Apple. Apple. Apple is in danger,' thought Birdie, and she opened the sitting-room door.

'Tinkle. Tinkle. Tinkle. Tinkle. Tinkle.' The sound

of the music met her so much more full and clear near the musical box that the sound of it knocked against the sound of Darner's barking in her head and confused her. She did not know she had come in; she could not see what was happening to Apple.

For Apple was standing on one of the tapestry chairs, which was dragged up near the table, and he was leaning over the lamp with his darning-wool wig near the candle flame; there was a strong smell of singeing, and it was just going to send the whole of Apple up in flames.

Marchpane was sitting on the couch, watching him and smiling her china smile.

'Tinkle. Tinkle,' went the musical box.

'Prrick!' barked Darner. 'Prrick! Prrick! Prrick! Prrrrrickkkckckckck!' he barked frantically.

'Isn't that Darner?' asked Tottie in the kitchen.

Marchpane went on watching, watching with her smile.

'It is Darner,' said Mr Plantaganet, and he dropped his newspaper.

'Emily!' said Charlotte suddenly. 'Something is happening in the dolls' house.'

'Tcha!' said Emily. She was not liking the dolls' house at present. They could hear the musical box,

'Tinkle. Tinkle. Tinkle. Tinkle.' 'Nonsense. What could happen?' asked Emily.

'I smell singeing,' said Charlotte, sniffing. 'Emily, did you light the birthday candle?'

'Prrick! Prrick! Prrrrrickkckckckck!' barked Darner so loudly that Birdie heard him clearly over the music.

'Darner. Tinkle. Darner. Tinkle,' fluttered Birdie, while Marchpane smiled. 'What am I to do?' cried Birdie. 'Which is it? Is it which?'

'P-R-I-C-K!' barked Darner.

As the candle caught the edge of Apple's fringe and he screamed, as Tottie and Mr Plantaganet tumbled in at the door, and Emily and Charlotte swung open the dolls' house front, the sound of Apple's scream tore the sound of Darner's barking and the tinkling music out of Birdie's head. She had one thought, and she threw herself at the lamp.

'Birdie! Back! Back! Back!' cried Mr Plantaganet.

'Birdie! Let me!' screamed Tottie. 'Birdie, you are made of celluloid, remember!'

'Celluloid!' said Birdie in her light calm voice, and the lightness of the real candle was in her face. Light as she was, she threw herself between Apple and the lamp, and Apple fell off the chair face downward on the carpet and put out the spark of fire in his wig.

There was a flash, a bright light, a white flame, and where Birdie had been there was no more Birdie, no sign of Birdie at all, only, sinking gradually down on the carpet beside Apple, floated Birdie's clothes, burning, slowly turning brown, and going into holes; last of all, the fire ran up the pink embroidery cotton of her apron strings and they waved up in the air, as they used to wave on Birdie, and then were burnt right up.

'Tinkle. Tinkle. Tinkle,' said the musical box.

Marchpane smiled.

# Chapter 21

'But where did Birdie go?' asked Charlotte.

'She was celluloid. That is highly inflammable,' said Father.

'What is "highly inflammable"?'

'It burns up in a flash, leaving nothing behind it.'

'Birdie left nothing behind,' said Charlotte sadly.

'But what happened? What happened? I still don't understand what happened,' said Mr Plantaganet.

'Apple was standing on the chair far too near the lamp. You must have put him there, Charlotte,' said Emily.

'I didn't,' said Charlotte.

'Don't be silly, Charlotte,' said Emily. 'And his wig must have caught fire. That was what we smelled singeing; and we opened the front so quickly that we tumbled Tottie and Mr Plantaganet over, and Birdie was standing too near, though I have warned you, Charlotte, and they tumbled her over so that she fell against the lamp and knocked Apple over, and was burned herself.'

'She gave her life for Apple,' said Charlotte.

'What a good thing it was only Birdie,' said Emily, but she did not say it very certainly.

'She gave her life for Apple.'

'I suppose she did in a way. I suppose – if you like to call it that.'

'She gave her life for Apple.'

'Don't go on and on, Charlotte.'

'Tottie tumbled in at the door,' said Charlotte, 'and Mr Plantaganet did too. I put them in the kitchen. I didn't put them in the doorway, although you say I did. I didn't put them there nor Apple on the chair, nor, nor – Birdie near him. The only one who never moved,' said Charlotte loudly, 'was Marchpane.'

'Yes, Marchpane,' said Emily slowly.

'I should like to take her up by a pair of tongs,' said Charlotte, 'and drop her in the fire.'

'Oh, Charlotte. She is far too beautiful.'

'She isn't beautiful at all,' said Charlotte. 'She is nasty and she smells nasty too. She isn't beautiful.' A thought struck her. 'Emily,' she said, 'wasn't Birdie beautiful when she went up in that flame? Like a fairy, like a beautiful kind of silver firework.'

'Birdie would have liked that,' said Emily, and she sounded like the old Emily who knew so well what all the Plantaganets liked. 'Oh, Charlotte!'

'Yes, Emily?'

'I – wish . . . '

'Yes, Emily?'

'I wish the dolls' house was like it was – before Marchpane.'

'Yes, Emily.'

'Suddenly,' said Emily, 'I don't like Marchpane very much.'

'Nor do I,' said Charlotte decidedly.

'I didn't like the way – she sat there – when Apple – when Birdie –'

'Nor did I,' said Charlotte.

'I'm sorry now,' said Emily. 'I wish – but what are we to do with her, Charlotte? She is too valuable and beautiful. We should never be allowed to throw her away. We must do something with her.'

'She must go out of the dolls' house,' said Charlotte. 'She must go out at once.'

Marchpane sat all this time on the couch, staring in front of her with her smile on her face, as if she had not heard a word, as if she were something stuffed in a glass case.

Perhaps it was that that put it into Charlotte's head. Charlotte who so seldom had ideas. This was Charlotte's idea, not Emily's, or perhaps it was Tottie's, for it came to Charlotte like a voice, and it might have been Tottie's voice. It was Tottie who knew how Marchpane had liked being at the cleaners, and at the Exhibition. Cleaners. Exhibition. The thought came clearly into Charlotte's head.

'I know,' said Charlotte. 'We must give her to a museum.'

# Chapter 22

Marchpane enjoyed being in the museum. She was in a glass case, between a lace collar and a china model of a King Charles spaniel. She was dusted very carefully twice a week and a number of people came to look at her. Sometimes young men and girls came to the museum to make drawings, and Marchpane was always quite sure, no matter what they drew, that they were making drawings of her. Every day she increased a little more in conceit, and the glass case made her safe from ever being played with.

# Chapter 23

Towards six o'clock, just after tea, Charlotte brought Mr Plantaganet back from the post office and put him in his chair in the sitting room and gave him his paper. Emily brought Tottie in from shopping; she had found Tottie a raffia shopping basket the size of a nut, and she made Tottie hang it up with her cloak in the hall. Then she went in to sit with Mr Plantaganet. Apple was upstairs. He had been sent to bed early by Tottie so that he could not play with the lamp. Charlotte still said she had not put him on the chair, and Emily had lately given

151

up saying that she had. Apple was safely in bed, tucked up in his patchwork quilt so that only his round head showed. Emily had clipped his burnt fringe straight with nail scissors and his plush had not been hurt at all. Darner lay quietly, snugly, in his kennel.

'Shall we let them have a little music?' asked Emily, and she wound up the musical box. It went 'tinkle, tinkle' and Darner stirred in his dreams.

Mr Plantaganet could not tell one of its tunes from the other. 'I have to have words,' said Mr Plantaganet. 'Words help me to know what it is. Like those carols, Tottie. Do you remember them?' And he began to hum 'God Bless the Master of This House'. 'Do you remember them, Tottie?'

'I remember everything,' said Tottie, listening to the music.

'Yes, I suppose you must, and for so long,' said Mr Plantaganet. 'Such a long time, Tottie.'

'Yes,' said Tottie.

'Things come and things pass,' said little Mr Plantaganet.

'Everything, from trees to dolls,' said Tottie.

'Even for small things like us, even for dolls. Good things and bad things, but the good things have come back, haven't they, Tottie?' asked Mr Plantaganet anxiously.

'Of course they have,' said Tottie in her kind wooden voice.

'Good things and bad. They were very bad,' said Mr Plantaganet.

'But they come and pass, so let us be happy now,' said Tottie.

'Without Birdie?' asked Mr Plantaganet, his voice trembling.

'Birdie would be happy. She couldn't help it,' said Tottie.

And Birdie's bright tinkling music went on in the dolls' house and, on her hat that still hung in the hall, and on her feather broom, and on her bird and on her parasol, the colours and patterns were still bright.